Butterfly

Butterfly

SONYA HARTNETT

CANDLEWICK PRESS

Copyright © 2009 by Sonya Hartnett

First U.S. edition 2010

First published by Penguin Group (Australia) 2009

Library of Congress Cataloging-in-Publication Data

Hartnett, Sonya.
Butterfly / Sonya Hartnett. —1st U.S. ed.
p. cm.
Summary: In 1980s Australia, nearly fourteen-year-old Ariella "Plum" Coyle fears the disapproval of her friends, feels inferior to her older brothers, and hates her awkward, adolescent body but when her glamorous neighbor befriends her, Plum starts to become what she wants to be — until she discovers her neighbor's ulterior motive.
ISBN 978-0-7636-4760-5
[1. Adolescence — Fiction. 2. Self-esteem — Fiction. 3. Interpersonal relations — Fiction. 4. Family life — Australia — Fiction. 5. Australia — Fiction.]
I. Title
PZ7.H267387But 2010
[Fic] — dc22   2009046549

10 11 12 13 14 15 16 BVG 10 9 8 7 6 5 4 3 2 1

Printed in Berryville, VA, U.S.A.

This book was typeset in Adobe Garamond.

Candlewick Press
99 Dover Street
Somerville, Massachusetts 02144

visit us at www.candlewick.com

For S. B.

PLUM IS SOON TO TURN FOURTEEN, and one evening she stands in front of a mirror with her school dress around her ankles, her body reflected naked and distressing in the glass. If her reflection is true then she has gone about in public like this — this thick black hair hugging her face like a sheenless scarf; these greasy cheeks with their evolving crop of scarlet lumps; this scurfy, hotly sunburned skin; these twin fleshy nubbins on her chest that are the worst things of all, worse than the downy hair that's feathered between her legs, worse than the specks of blackness blocking her pores, worse even than the womanly hurdle that still awaits her, the prospect of which occurrence makes her seize into silence — and nobody has informed her of the fact that she is hideous. Her reflection is so troubling that her gaze veers, seeking comfort in the posters tacked to the walls. One shows glossy kittens, another is David Bowie. She breathes deeply and lets a moment pass before sliding her sights back to the mirror. This is she, Ariella Coyle, aged thirteen. Carefully she scans her face, her shoulders, her waist, grimaces at the sight of a meaty bottom and thighs. Her hands gather her hair in a dense ponytail, and her face, unshielded, looks round and inflamed, her eyes the tarred tips of poison darts. Her arms are strong, her neck utilitarian, not vulnerable at all: indeed, Plum's entire body is somehow *too much*—too tall, too thriving, too *there*. Her stomach is the color of uncooked dough, and feels, when poked, like dough. *Ariella Coyle,* aged nearly fourteen, waylaid monstrously on the path to being grown. "There is no God," she tells her reflection: as quickly as that, she knows it is true. "And even if there *was* a God," she adds vindictively, "He wouldn't love you. Look at you. *Nobody* could love you."

The words should be like pools of blood, but the idea of such forsakenness actually makes Plum smile. Of late she's been attracted to all things ruthless and peculiar. She sometimes feels edgy and dangerous, like an animal with unblinking eyes. She's starting to think there might be something supernatural about her. She can guess what people are about to say, and when the telephone will ring; once, she heard her name spoken loudly behind her, though nobody was standing there. And yet, despite her superiority, Plum can never quite make herself immune to human needs. She can't quite make herself not care.

Her mother calls "Dinner" from downstairs, and Plum hears the word like a dog hears *walk*. She catches herself—her greed is infuriating—and points a finger at the mirror. "You eat too much. Don't eat so much. *Try.*" Her thoughts, these days, waltz obsessively around the subject of food—how much she might get, how long until she'll get more—and it's an obsession that is exhausting. So much about being almost fourteen is, in fact, so wearying that for an instant Plum feels light-headed with all she must endure. She has older brothers whose duty it is to tease her—if the situation requires, they'll find her taste in clothes and music and heartthrobs a source of crushing mirth. But lately Justin and Cydar have been keeping their opinions to themselves, and their silence rolls up Plum's spine like a hearse.

Mums calls, "Dinner!"

Plum kicks her uniform aside and takes from beneath her pillow a pair of baby-blue, lace-trimmed pajamas. Dressed, she checks the mirror, ensuring the worst is disguised. She hunches her shoulders, shakes out her hair, stoops her overgrown height. Her cheeks, in the summery dusk, in the anguished infancy of teenagerhood, are the pasty yellow of cereal left to float all day in milk.

The Coyle house is big, and humiliating. The staircase down which Plum runs is gloomy with pastoral paintings, hazardous with piled books. Nothing in the house is new: indeed, the more elderly an object, the more Mums and

Fa must possess it. On weekends they trawl antique shops, returning with chairs and statues and complicated wooden boxes. Before she'd known better, Plum had trawled with them; now she stays at home on weekends, curled on the couch watching science-fiction movies, and wishes she lived somewhere less mortifying. It's unfair that she must endure timber and stone, when all her friends know the joy of plastic and smoked glass. The dinner table to which she's been called is a lengthy slab of wood over which drunken friars might have drooled inside murky taverns. The seats are two ungiving pews salvaged from a church. It is embarrassing to ask a friend to dinner when they won't have their own separate chair, rude to expect anyone to use ivory-handled cutlery to eat from crazed china plates at a table that should have been torched. Plum's wildest dream is to have her bedroom carpeted in white shag—walls, ceiling, door, floor, all pristinely white and furry. The possession she craves more than anything is a miniature television—not one cased in wood, like the one in the den, but set inside a sphere of chrome, with three stumpy legs and a rapier-like aerial. She has seen such a thing in a shop, and it made her feel strangely like weeping.

Plum slides into place on a pew, skidding sideways to let Justin sit beside her. He pinches her arm as he sits down, and she pinches him back harder, her heart fattening with love. Rangy as a tall ship, handsome as a prince's portrait, a power of aliveness radiates from Justin the way light beams away from the stars. To Plum he is without flaw, a kind of sun-king. He works behind the counter of a bottle shop, and has earned enough to buy a Holden as big as a barge. Occasionally he drives Plum to school in it, dropping her off by the side gate where the tough girls smoke before assembly. It is often the only moment of her day when Plum feels all is not lost. "*Planet of the Apes* tonight," she reminds him, but he shakes his head, says, "Can't." She whines and screws her face up, but he just reaches for the water jug. "You've seen it before. You've seen it a hundred times. If you watch it again you'll *turn into* an ape." Fa comes in from the den then, half-asleep and rubbing the ear that's been compressed by the transistor, and Justin turns to him gladly. "What's the score?"

"Australia six for ninety at stumps. Border not out on forty."

"We're going to lose."

"We'll be cooked like a curry!"

"What about Imran?"

Justin's eyes flash toward Plum. Fa says, "Imran went out for nine."

"Plummy loves Imran."

"I don't!" Plum denies. "He's just good."

"Where's Cydar?" asks Mums, passing out slabs of plate; and suddenly Cydar is there in the room, a hawk whistled down from the sky. He drops into his place opposite Plum like a sheet snapping on the wind. Cydar is the middle child, shy-eyed and secretive, a breeder of night-life-colored fish which he sells to men who don't talk. He keeps himself and his aquariums in a weathered bungalow at the end of the garden, where he is visited by acquaintances as languid as the fish. He is studying at university something to do with microscopes, something that makes Plum proud but bored. She thinks he should be a rock star—he has that wastrel look. He should play Judas in *Jesus Christ Superstar*. Cydar has a girlfriend, Justin once claimed, about whom they must never speak. "Why not?" Plum had asked; and Justin explained, "Because she has no reflection. Because her eyes are white. Because she can only eat what she's killed with her bare hands. Don't say her name! You'll summon her."

Cydar's gaze had merely glided away, as if there was so much he could say in retaliation that it was most satisfying to say nothing. Now he says, "I thought you loved that other one. Pascoe."

"I don't love any of them! Pascoe's all right."

"Big bad Lenny," contemplates Fa.

"A girl at school has his name all over her folder. *Lenny Pascoe, Lenny Pascoe,* about ten thousand times. I like his hair," Plum admits.

Mums sits down beside Cydar, polite distance between their elbows. "Hot pot," says Justin approvingly, lifting the lid from the casserole dish; he is not home for dinner often enough to notice the frequency with which his mother serves this meal, as if she's discovered, running beneath the kitchen's tiles, a seam of sausage and segmented pineapple. Plum, however, decides stoutly, "Mums, I don't want that.

I'm not eating hot pot ever again. It's fattening. I'm fat."

"Poo," says her mother, which means many things, none of them being that Plum may not eat. She shifts the lid from a sarcophagus of rice, releasing a curse of steam. "Imran caught off Chappell for nine," Fa reflects dreamily; he comes alive to ask "How's the car?" of Justin, who's been tinkering in the driveway all afternoon.

"The starter motor is soon to be kaput."

Fa frowns with sympathy or possibly confusion; Justin, reminded, waves beneath Plum's nose a knuckle he has skinned with a spanner. "Get away!" she squeals, swatting with her knife. "That's revolting! Mums, Justin is being revolting! You're revolting, Justin!"

"Revolting!" He's pleased. Cydar, who this morning sold a glimmering finned creature for the fantastic sum of fifty dollars, who can feel the note and all its potential in the hip pocket of his jeans, who will never spend a single minute of his life laboring over a car, says, "You're driving it tonight though, aren't you? I don't want to catch a taxi."

"Where are you going?"

"Away from you."

"To the pub, I bet! When you could be watching *Planet of the Apes* . . ."

Fa has turned to Cydar now. "How are the fish doing?"

"Swimmingly," says Cydar.

"You know what I'd like to see?" Justin elbows his sister. "A battle between the gorillas from *Planet of the Apes* and the skeleton warriors from *Jason and the Argonauts*."

"The gorillas would win. They're stronger."

"But those skeletons are dodgy. *And* they've got spears."

Fa asks, "How was school today, old Plummy?"

Plum answers offhandedly, "All right." School is an endurance test for her, a situation she faces like a brick wall every day, but she seldom answers anything but *good*. She knows precise things about her father — that he works with numbers, prefers his eggs cooked through, has a plate in an ankle from a boyhood broken bone — but there is an obscuring fog of softness around him that Plum is wary of disturbing with truths that aren't *good*. Her father catches a tram at ten past eight each weekday morning, taking a seat where he can see the tram's wide door slipped open and closed by the grade of the road. "Why do you watch the door?" she'd asked once, expecting an answer about mathematics or time; instead Fa had replied, "It rests me." And the words had terrified Plum, because what they implied was terrifying; and she'd vowed never to expose, or expose herself to, such wistfulness again. For this same reason, Plum will never ask her mother what she thinks about when she's alone in the house and it's raining, those cold afternoons when Plum arrives home to find Elvis gazing up from record sleeves shuffled over the floor. It is one thing for Plum to exist on the edge of desolation: but the thought of anyone in her family being anything less than happy fills her head with the noise of an untuned radio. She longs to shout at Fa, *You've got what you're supposed to have!* A job, a house, children, a wife. *What else do you want?*

Sometimes she almost hates him for being the way he is.

Anyway, it is Plum's growing conviction that a mother and a father have no right to feelings. A parent should be a person the way a door is a door, something like the robot in *Lost in Space*—loving and providing and cleaning, not distracted by wishes and needs. The only thing that really matters about a parent is the existence of the child. If Mums and Fa ever were fourteen, they're well beyond it now; beyond the time when their lives are vital things. Even when they were fourteen, it's unlikely that they had problems as grievous as Plum's.

And now everyone is talking about something that doesn't concern her, scooping out globes of fuzzy rice, shunting the water jug down the table. Justin and Cydar are deciding what time they should leave, and Justin thinks the car will need petrol; Fa is saying he'll build shelves in the kitchen to accommodate Mums's collection of jelly molds. Mums has picked up a dropped cluster of rice and the sticky grains are clinging like grubs to her fingers, won't be shaken onto her plate. "Trouble is," she's saying, "you're not a *builder*. Everything you build *falls down* . . ." And all of it is so unworthy of being spoken at all.

"Listen!" Plum barks. "Everyone be quiet. I have something important to say. I'm not going to church anymore."

It's a decision she's hardly known she has made, coming upon her like the urge to burp. Immediately, however, she's committed. Having released the words, she's relieved. "All right?"

Across the table Mums's mouth twists, as if her daughter is something bitter she'd expected to be sweet. "Plum."

"Justin doesn't go. Cydar doesn't. Fa never did. Why should I?"

"You *need* to." Justin stabs a stump of sausage with a hundred-year-old fork. "You're unholy. You've got horns on your head."

Plum pauses — she's seen people-beasts in movies with horns on their heads, and thinks the look charismatic. Horns would change her life. "Well," she says, "I'm not going. God's never done anything for *me*. And I don't believe in Him."

Mums clicks her tongue. "Don't say that at the table."

"Why not at the table?" But Cydar is ignored.

"You can't make me." Plum is captured by strange determination. This is what she is supposed to do, now that she's nearly fourteen and the docility of childhood is behind her. She is meant to start becoming what she wants to be. "If I don't believe in God, it's stupid to go to church. It's hypothetical."

"It's what?" says Cydar.

Fa says, "What's made you stop believing in God, Plummo?"

Plum's head pivots. There is no overhead lamp and the table is lit only by what light vaults the kitchen counter, so Fa sits in shadows. "I never did. I've always thought it was silly." She speaks with certainty, although what she says isn't strictly true. As a child, she'd believed: but believing is what children do. "Look at it sensibly. The whole thing doesn't make sense. If God is real, where did He come from? And what about the dinosaurs—how come they weren't in the Garden of Eden? And why do bad things happen, if God is so kind? And how come, if God made everything, everything can be explained by something that *isn't* God, something that's *normal*—"

Cydar says, "It's called science."

"It's common sense!" shrills Plum. "Angels and Hell and Satan and Heaven—only a *kid* would believe that stuff! Only somebody who wasn't brave, or wasn't—*educated*—or wasn't—modern! And *I'm* not a kid!"

"You are," says Justin. "You're a little goat. Those horns."

"I've grown up!" Plum squawks; then quickly rounds her shoulders lest the ludicrous nubbins show and it's assumed she's referring to them. "I'm nearly fourteen!"

"Are you going to have a party?" asks Fa. "For your birthday?"

Plum glares at him, distracted. "What? I don't know. I haven't decided. I'm not talking about that—"

"Parties are for kids," Cydar suggests.

"No they're not! That's a stupid thing to say. Justin had a party when he was twenty-one." The occasion is one of Plum's most satisfying memories, Justin's crowds of fabulous friends and the noisy fuss they'd made of young Plum; the highlight had come when a female guest fainted, and Fa had tapped her face until she revived. "Everyone's having slumber parties. Can I have one, Mums?"

Her mother looks tortured, which means her daughter may. The girl scrambles upright on the pew. "I want everything bought from the supermarket—nothing homemade. I want mini pizzas and chicken wings, and cashews and macaroons. An ice-cream cake from a cake shop, not some horrible sponge. No balloons or streamers or games either. And punch instead of soft drink—"

"And bags of lollies to take home?"

Plum's lip hoists. "We're *fourteen,* Justin. You don't get bags of lollies at our age."

"Do you giggle about boys instead?"

It's the kind of brotherly comment that makes Plum feel like a deer in a huntsmen's forest. She glances past the casserole dish to where Cydar sits in dimness, wrists bent above his plate. She does not need light to know his eyes are still and cool on her. "None of your business. We'll talk about whatever we want. You're not invited, so you'll never know."

Cydar says nothing, which is more disconcerting than words. Mums is standing to saw slices from the lumpy loaf. "And what do you want as a present?"

The miniature television in its globe of chrome flames like a star in Plum's mind, blinding Cydar from sight. The television is, without question, the most desirable item she's ever seen. None of her friends have a TV to themselves, let alone one so enviable. Nor, Plum suspects, will she, for its price tag had made her swing away, swallowing with disappointment. Her family isn't poor, but some things are beyond the realm of reasonable expectation. Nevertheless she has cleared a space on top of her dresser, to prove that the object would fit. She has lain on her bed and imagined watching the pint-sized screen. "I don't know," she mumbles; to her horror, tears are close. She has seen herself unwrapping a television-sized box on the morning of her birthday; she's accompanied herself to school, casually announced the new possession, reveled in the envious mewls of her friends. She's constructed a new and entirely perfect life around something that is, in reality, as unattainable as Everest's peak. It's the kind of make-believe thing a child would do, as poignant as a broken heart. Indeed, Plum feels her heart *is* breaking over the loss of what never was. She dredges her voice past a clot of grief that has bulged inside her throat. "The only thing I want is something you won't let me have. I won't even bother telling you what it is, because I know I won't get it."

"Oh no," Justin sighs. "Not another bloody pony?"

Tears, humiliated and humiliating, spurt from Plum's eyes: she throws down her cutlery and struggles to her feet. "Shut up!" she wails. "You always laugh at me! I'm a *person,* I have *feelings,* I'm not a *joke*! Why can't you all just *leave me alone*?"

And having clambered over the back of the pew Plum departs the table, pounding through the house like a rock down a cliffside, storming up the stairs like a centurion.

༈ IN HER BEDROOM she drops to her knees, reaching into the darkness beneath her bed for the handle of an old briefcase, which she pulls into the light with such aggravated force that the case leaps like a seal into her lap. The latches snap open militarily, *chock chock,* and as Plum lifts the lid her breath comes out snotty and rasped. She gazes upon the case's contents with an archaeologist's eye: here lies her treasure, her most sacred things. She has lined the briefcase with lavender satin and provided several bags' worth of cotton-ball cushioning so that each token sits within its own bulky cloud, untroubled by her manhandling of the case. Plum brushes the items with her palm, incanting as she does so a string of whispery words. The glass lamb. *I belong.* The Fanta yo-yo. *Admire me.* The jade three dark stars align—makes her rise and spread her awesome wings; and then the whole world, gulping, will understand.

"Her, her, her," she bawls, chewing heroically.

Her eyes are pinched closed, but when she hears her name spoken they flip open with surprise. The evening sky is marlin-blue and pink, extraordinarily beautiful; the breeze that fiddles in her hair is as jestful as a sprite. Her name flutters around her like the skeleton of a leaf—*Plum, Plum, Plum*—uttered in the hushed but unswerving voice of the Underworld. Plum is so startled that she stops both chewing and howling, the chocolate turning to clay in her mouth. For all she has daydreamed, she's never believed, but suddenly she's rigid with what's true. There are no angels, but there *are* demons, and one of them has come for her. And suddenly Plum would rather be ordinary after all.

"Plum? Are you hurt?"

Her sights plunge toward the ground, over the fence and into the garden of the house next door, where their neighbor stands with her hands clutched together, peering up troubledly. "Can I help you? You're so sad."

Plum's face scalds. The Coyle family is not on such personal terms with the people next door that the woman—whose name, *Maureen Wilks,* Plum knows, but little else, and nor does she want to—may take the liberty of intruding in this way. The Coyles have lived in this street forever, their Wilks neighbors for only a few years, qualifying Plum to regard them with the hoitiness of landed gentry. She tucks the MARS Bar out of sight, smears her eyes with the flat of a hand. "I'm fine," she says, infusing each word with enough curtness and weight to impact into the earth. "I'm not—sad."

Maureen Wilks considers her openly, so Plum feels her gaze like probing fingers. She would back into the darkness of her room, heave the window and pull the blind shudderingly, if only that would not appear rude the way this spying lady is rude, staring and listening and intruding. "You look like Rapunzel in her tower," the woman says. "Standing up there, waiting for a prince to rescue you."

Plum bridles: Rapunzel is her most-scorned distressed damsel. Those coils of moldery moth-eaten hair, the idiocy in never thinking of lowering herself to the ground, rather than waiting to be climbed. "Do I?" she answers uncivilly.

The neighbor steps forward, her shadow skimming the fence. Her head is tipped to see Rapunzel, and Plum can see down her cleavage. "Would you like to come to David's party, Plum? We're having a picnic. There's plenty of food, and we've filled the pool, but there are no guests except me."

Plum's window is high enough to overlook every corner of the neighboring garden, and she notices now, in the shade of a tree, the small boy lying on his stomach in a shallow wading pool. She's seen him in the garden before, breaking twigs, investigating. Laid out on a rug at a safe distance from the pool are platters of food that say only *childhood:* triangles of bread dotted with hundreds-and-thousands, frankfurters pierced with wooden toothpicks, lemony cupcakes and bowls of Smarties, bottles of garish fizz. Every immature morsel Plum has banished from her own party; everything she's loved, and still does. Though caramel yet clings to her teeth, her heart longs for cupcake, her heart demands fizz. "Is it David's birthday?"

"Yes; he's four. Please come. His father's away, there's only me. He would love to have a guest. Wouldn't you, David?"

David, startled by inclusion, dips his face into the water. Plum hesitates, naturally antisocial: but her desire for the party food is like the tug of a clutching hand. She needs a frankfurter, she pines for sparkling drink. In the space of mere moments she could be sitting on a rug, being six years old again. And if her mother opens the door, she will find her daughter's room deserted. Plum's absence will first puzzle, then worry her family, and make them think back on how they've treated her. "I'll come," she says. "Wait a minute."

She shuts the window and quickly changes out of her pajamas, pulling on a T-shirt and a pair of toweling shorts. From a shelf she takes a picture book that has no place in her heart. *Dear David,* she writes on its opening page. *Happy . . .* She doesn't know whether it's forth or fourth. *Dear David, Happy birthday. Love from your neighbor Miss Ariella "Plum" Coyle.* Underneath this she adds the elaborate flourish she's been practicing of late. Then she creeps downstairs, book under her arm, Roman sandals soundless on the uncarpeted stairs. She hears her parents and brothers talking at the dinner table — Plum would like to know if they're discussing her, and pauses: then hearing laughter, complicated and conniving, hurries on as if shoveled. She feeds herself through the querulous screen door, then speeds across the summer-sharp lawn to the footpath, rounds the fence that divides her house from the next, and trots up the neighboring driveway. And it's only now that Plum remembers all those naive little girls tempted into vans or past a front door, lured by lollies or the promise of a puppy, never to be seen again. The recollection slows her, rolls her eyes in her head. The evening seems unnaturally quiet, her home suddenly far away. Yet she cannot turn back, she's committed herself now, and if Plum must vanish she's already vanished, and her great destiny was only to become a legendary lost girl. "Hello?" She passes through the side gate with her heart like an anvil. "I'm here — hello?"

The little boy, David, has left the wading pool and is standing on the lawn with his arms held out, his body shining bluely with water. His mother is kneeling close to him, drying his back with a towel. At the sight of Plum, the boy twines his feet and smiles. His smile is oddly graceful, and makes Plum feel confused. Looking away, she sees that the garden is different to how it appears from the height of her window. There's a flowery scent, and the coolness of damp, and the ticking of leaf against leaf; most weirdly, everything seems stretched skyward, making her think of fairies and of sleepy tumbles down rabbit holes. She looks past the fence to her bedroom window—how peculiar to think that, moments ago, she had been standing so forlornly at the sill. She wonders if Rapunzel, returned to the ground, looked up at her tower and realized it was not what she had believed. That she could have jumped.

"Here's our guest!" The mother, Mrs. Wilks, rises, smiling at Plum. "You see, David, I told you someone would come. Now we can have a proper party!"

Plum hands over her gift. "Happy birthday, David. Sorry, I didn't have wrapping paper."

"Oh, a book! How kind! David, what do you say?"

David says, "I got a truck."

Plum doesn't consider herself good with children, nor does she find them endearing. She resents their chaos, their self-absorption, their compulsive stealing of the limelight. This child, however, is like a shy little calf, and glances away sweetly when Plum meets his eye. "What sort of truck?" she asks; and the boy heaves a sigh and says, "A Tonka truck."

"A Tonka truck!" Plum plucks a tidbit from a past she wasn't part of, wanting the boy to think well of her. "My brothers had Tonka trucks when they were little."

"Did you hear that, David? Justin and Cydar had Tonka trucks too."

It surprises the girl to hear her brothers' names fall so familiarly from the woman's mouth, but at once it is understandable: neighbors know the names of neighbors. Maureen Wilks had known Plum's name, and Plum somehow knows hers. The whole world is joined, like a dot-to-dot, by someone knowing somebody else's name. Her inclusion in this intricate web fills Plum with a warm sense of humanity's oneness. The night is beautiful, the world is beautiful, and for all her imperfections Plum is included and wanted. For a moment, she is happier than she's ever been.

They settle on the tartan rug, the platters laid out between them. Plum says loudly to the boy, "What a lot of food! Were you expecting a king?" The child looks at her blankly; Mrs. Wilks passes out paper plates. "Everyone help themselves," she invites. David takes a frankfurter and a cupcake: "Frankfurter first," his mother instructs. Plum blots tomato sauce onto her plate and selects a party pie. Mrs. Wilks fills three mugs with creamy soda—Plum can't decide if there were always three cups, or if the lady fetched a third from the kitchen while Plum was changing out of her pajamas. Mosquitoes arrive and wobble about; Mrs. Wilks sprays her son's arms and feet with repellent, and then, laughing, does the same for Plum. The smell of the food, the tingle of spray, the scratch of the rug, the taste of the toothpicks, the hiss of the soda which is like bubbly snake venom—all these mingle in the February dusk into something that is the essence of childhood, feels exactly as the best days of Plum's childhood felt. And she's stricken with sudden nostalgia for the life she's been so eager to pack away, she wishes there was some way of being everything at once—grown and sure and clever, young and protected and new.

They eat in silence for a time, the song of the cicadas

rising, the sparrows hurrying to roost. Mrs. Wilks sweeps her palms through the grass, David spills soda on the rug. A fragile mosquito bogs itself in Plum's tomato sauce — Maureen says, "Poor thing," and picks it out with a fingernail. Plum notices that David is choosing from the platters the same morsels she chooses for herself, then studiously watches how she eats them — one bite, one sip, several ruminative chews — and eats the same way himself. She throws a Smartie into her mouth, gulps it down like a pelican; shyly, the boy tries the same. She juggles two Cheezels but he won't attempt this, only gives her his cautious smile.

Mrs. Wilks says eventually, "I've eaten too much." She leans on her hands and tilts her face to the sky, closing her eyes in a way that makes Plum a little embarrassed. "I love the last days of summer. There's so much . . . *poignancy* in the air. As if summer were a living thing that's drifting gently into death. Don't you think so, Plum?"

Plum says, "I guess."

"There's an owl living in that big melaleuca near the fence — she's quiet in winter, but she hoots through these mild nights. Do you ever hear her?"

"No," says Plum; then, dissatisfied, changes it to, "Sometimes."

"Look at the moon, David." The lady's eyes glide open, she raises a sculptured hand to the disc above their heads. "And that bright twinkling dot isn't a star — it's a planet. It's Venus, I think — is it Venus, Plum?"

"Maybe." Plum struggles.

"A huge mighty planet, tinier than an ant! Isn't that amazing, David?"

"I have this idea." Plum shuffles forward. "I think we should change the name of the planet Uranus. Nobody likes that name, so we should change it."

"What should we change it to?"

"We should change it to *Velvet*—"

"Velvet! That's perfect! Mercury, Venus, Earth, Mars, Jupiter, Saturn, Velvet, Neptune, Pluto. Much prettier!"

Plum grins. She feels welcome and pacified here, and wishes she'd brought a better book. But then Mrs. Wilks says quietly, "I hope you're not still sad?" and Plum's cheeks inflame. She would rather not speak of the spectacle she'd made of herself at the window. So often, of late, she finds herself ashamed to reflect on her behavior. It's ridiculous that a miniature television could reduce her to sobs, regrettable that the subject of her birthday is now tainted with shouts and sulks. Yet Plum owes this woman something for her kindness, and makes herself reply, "I wasn't sad—not really. Sometimes my family makes me angry, that's all."

Mrs. Wilks smiles. "I think that's what families are supposed to do, Plum. My family used to make me so angry that I dreamed about burning the house down, with them inside it."

Plum chuckles obligingly. "I don't want to do *that*," she says. "I just wish they'd remember I'm not a baby anymore. I'm nearly fourteen. I'm having a party, too," she adds. "Not like this one—a slumber party."

"Did you hear that, David? Plum is having a party too, a grown-up party. The thing is, Plum, you *are* the baby—you'll always be their baby, even when you're old and married, even when you're *much* older than fourteen."

"Hmm." Plum knows this, and privately finds it comforting. "It doesn't mean they should treat me like a kid, though. They never take me seriously. They act like I don't know what I'm talking about."

Her neighbor nods, and Plum sees that she is thoughtfully considering the complaint, not laughing it aside as Plum's mother would. Mrs. Wilks is quite a beautiful woman, in an Ali MacGraw, midday-movie kind of way. She is, perhaps, the same age as some of Plum's teachers, which is oldish but not *old*. Her face has no creases, her skin is smooth. Her hair is long, lustrously dark and fashionably flicked. Her eyes, also dark, are also quite long, and heavy with green shadow. She wears a turquoise, ruffle-sleeved dress which has geometrical shapes printed across it. The material clings to her flat stomach and lean thighs. For some reason Plum thinks of a word she's only heard used about the weather: *sultry*. "You think they don't respect you," Mrs. Wilks is saying. "They don't respect your decisions."

"That's right!" Plum sits up straighter, charged by the exactness of the phrase. "They don't respect my decisions! I think I'm old enough to stay home alone at night, but Mums says I'm not. When I wanted more pocket money, Mums said I don't need it. Whenever I go out, I have to say where I'm going and when I'll be home. And look at me — I'm fat. But when I told Mums I didn't want dinner, she *made* me eat it, even though I'm fat! I'm not even allowed to decide what to eat!"

"You're not fat—"

"I am! Look at me! I'm a whale!"

The intrusion of this subject causes instant dejection, turns the whole evening monochrome. Mrs. Wilks, however, laughs, although not as Mums would. She laughs like someone who knows what is true. "That's puppy fat, Plum. I had puppy fat too, at your age."

"But I'm ugly," Plum sulks. "You're not ugly."

"Ugly!" Mrs. Wilks claps her hands. "Who told you that? Only yourself, I bet. You're not ugly, Plum. You have nice olive skin. You're already tall. You have rich thick hair, a pure jet color. You've got good bones in your face. You've got a straight nose and a friendly smile and interesting eyes. You're exactly the type of girl who could become a fashion model."

Plum balks as though bitten. "Really?"

"Absolutely. You have the features that fashion photographers look for. You should never think you're ugly. You could be in magazines."

Plum lists sideways, dazed. Color is streaming back into the world — enough, and then too much, so the grass is emerald, the sky is mercury, the rug a circus of scarlet and sapphire. The lady's smile lingers on her; then she looks at her son. "Is it time for the candles, David?"

Disturbed into life, the child chirps, "Yes!"

"It's time for the cake." Maureen finds her feet like a turquoise doe. David is quick to follow his mother, so Plum is left sitting alone. In private she runs her fingers around the good bones of her face, up the steep slope of her nose, into her rich jet hair. Maybe things are not so terrible as she has believed. Magically, her body already feels less heavy, less sweaty and sluggish. When Mrs. Wilks emerges from the house with the cake, Plum looks at her with something like first love.

The candles are lit and the song is sung; Mrs. Wilks sings the *smell like a monkey* version. David huffs air on the four trembling flames, his mother and guest applaud. Mrs. Wilks slices three wedges of chocolate sponge, and again the partygoers dine in silence. There is not much light left in the clouds now, and the sky is empty of birds; mosquitoes hover needfully at the fringe of the picnic rug. Maureen refreshes the repellent on her son, then beckons Plum nearer so she too may be doused. The droplets sizzle on the girl's sunburned cheeks; she can't remember the last time her own mother sprayed her with insect repellent. Sucking cream from under her fingernails, Plum gazes around the garden, druggedly content. "It's much better here than at home."

"Life is difficult at your age," Mrs. Wilks replies. "Everything is fierce, and usually wrong."

It isn't the answer Plum had expected—yet it is also pristine. To be so deeply understood makes Plum's gaze go watery, and she has to glance away. "Shall I tell you something dreadful that happened to me when I was your age?" asks Mrs. Wilks.

"All right."

"One day, my mother took me to the doctor. My mother knew nothing, or nothing she'd admit to knowing — hardly anyone's mother did, in those days. So when I got a lumpy chest, she took me to the doctor. Maybe she thought I had a disease — maybe she just couldn't bear to explain. The doctor prodded and squeezed with his hairy hands. Our old family doctor, whom I'd known all my life, kneading away. Then he looked at my mother and said, *Your daughter is going to be a big girl*."

Plum pauses. "I don't get it."

"A *big girl*. I wasn't ill, I didn't have a disease. I was only growing breasts."

The word alone makes Plum hunch her shoulders around the upstarts on her own chest. She never talks about them, their arrival has gone unmentioned in her house: so it's alarming, yet also interesting, to hear this woman speak so openly of hers. "That must have been embarrassing."

"I nearly died."

"A big girl." Plum thinks on it, and gurgles.

"I came home and cried and cried. I was so angry. I felt utterly *betrayed*. No one had betrayed me, but that's how I felt. It's difficult, isn't it, being young? Nothing is easy, not for years."

This sobers Plum. "Not for years?"

"Not for me—not for many people. Not for years."

"But it's better now?" Plum suggests.

Mrs. Wilks shrugs. "Better in some ways. Not in every way."

Plum's eyebrows knit; she thinks of her father, his aggravating sadness. She can't understand this thread of dissatisfaction that pulls through perfect worlds. "You're married," she points out. "You're pretty."

"Things like that don't make the difference, Plum. You'll find out."

Plum, silenced, looks down at the ruined feast. The mugs are empty, the plates smeared, the fairy bread curling at the corners. David sits without a sound, his hands knotted in his lap. The girl feels the onus to say something wise. "If people aren't happy with what they have," she tries, "they should just change things, until they have what they want."

Mrs. Wilks smiles. Her eyes are two sleepy panthers that wake up when she smiles. "I wish it were that simple, Plum—maybe it is, and I just haven't realized. We should be friends, you and me, shouldn't we? It would make life happier—it would for me, anyway. We could be sisters. I could teach you about clothes and makeup. You could tell me your worries. It might be the saving of both of us."

And although Plum has never wanted a sister nor understood why anyone would, for the second time this evening she finds herself accepting an invitation she can't politely refuse. "OK," she has to say. Then the prospect of being privy to what this stylish woman knows presents itself like a key: "Yes, OK!"

"It will be fun," says Mrs. Wilks.

Plum has another creamy soda, Maureen has a cup of coffee. David wanders off through the trees, carrying the book that Plum gave him. Plum hears the back door of her house bang shut, then the rasping hinges of Cydar's bungalow door. Mums will be stacking the dinner dishes, Fa will be filling the sink. "I should go home," she supposes.

And with that, piercingly, her fear returns—this is the instant her neighbor will say, *You can't go home, you'll never go home.* Instead Mrs. Wilks says, "Thank you so much for coming. David was so pleased."

Plum's heart beats again. "Thank you for inviting me, Mrs. Wilks."

"*Mrs. Wilks!* That's not who I am. Please, Plum, call me Maureen. I can't bear old *Mrs. Wilks.*"

"OK," says Plum, who's honored.

"And what's happening at your house tonight? Will it be as quiet as ours?"

Plum says, "I'll be watching *Planet of the Apes.* It's one of my favorites. Roddy McDowall plays Cornelius, he's really good. It's not my *favorite* favorite, though. My favorite favorite is *The Omega Man.*"

"So you're a film buff?"

Plum shrugs modestly. "I guess. I like silly science-fiction movies best—*Journey to the Center of the Earth, Fantastic Voyage,* things like that. Ones where they get a little lizard and turn it into a monster. I like scary movies too—*The Exorcist* is my favorite, so is *Night of the Living Dead.* I also like those black-and-white horrors from the fifties—"

"Those ones about communism?"

"No, not about communism—about giant ants and swamp creatures and flying saucers. They're not scary—they're funny."

Maureen nods, the panthers sleep. "I don't know anything about movies. Maybe you can teach me. I know Alfred Hitchcock, that's all."

"Hitchcock is great! My favorite is *The Birds.* Most people's favorite is *Psycho,* but that's not his best. *North by Northwest* is his best, although some people reckon *Vertigo* is better. But *The Birds* is really good. You should watch it, if it comes on TV. But it's *Planet of the Apes* tonight. Usually Justin watches with me—his favorites are *Soylent Green* and *Enter the Dragon.* There's a coincidence between *Soylent Green* and *Planet of the Apes* and *The Omega Man*—do you know what it is?"

"I have no idea. Tell me."

"Charlton Heston stars in all of them. His most famous film is *Ben-Hur.* Justin says he's not a good actor, but I think he is. But Justin's going out with Cydar tonight, so I'll be watching *Planet of the Apes* by myself. You should watch it too, if you're not doing anything else."

"All right, I will. And where do your brothers go, on a Friday night? Out on dates?"

"I don't know." Plum staggers upright, shedding crumbs. "They don't tell me anything I can tease them about."

Maureen laughs. It's a lovely, silky sound. "I'm so glad we're friends," she says. "I'll learn a lot from you."

"I'm glad too."

"Listen—I've had a small idea, one that might help you. I suppose you always take your lunch to school?"

Plum nods, distracted by a wodge of cream on her sleeve. "Mums makes sandwiches."

"Well, then, if you want to lose weight, why don't you put your lunch in the bin? Monday to Friday, in the bin. Your mother won't know, so she won't worry. You'll be slimmer in no time."

Plum frowns down at her. "I've never thought of that."

"You should try it. It will work. And one other thing: your real name surely isn't Plum?"

"No." The girl hesitates. "It's stupid. It's Ariella."

"Ariella! Beautiful! I've never heard a more beautiful name. Stop calling yourself Plum—it's absurd, you're not a fruit!—and start calling yourself Ariella—no, *Aria*! Aria, like a song. Live life as Aria from now on: *be* Aria, *think* Aria. Trust me, it will make a difference."

And Plum, dazzled, trusts her, and believes. She goes home that night remade. Even the discomfort of her stomach, a drum swollen convex with sugar and gas, doesn't prevent her from feeling she's found her necessary wings.

SATURDAY IS HOT BY SUNRISE, and will be fiery by midday. Plum wakes full of a child's Christmas Eve glee. She has made, last night, a new and powerful friend: all awkwardness and uncertainty are behind her now. When Fa brings her breakfast—sweet tea, unstrained, so she can drink the leaves; thick toast, unsliced and heavily buttered, all tumors excised from the strawberry jam—she says, "Thanks very much, Fa," with such feeling that he is stopped in his tracks. "That's all right, Plummy," he says. And it would be too mean to correct him: *Aria*.

When she's eaten her breakfast Plum untangles her sheets and crosses the room to pull up the blind. The morning sunlight drives her backward, making her blink dramatically. Leaning into the glass, she sees something that tears away the edges of her good mood. Parked in the driveway of the house next door is the Datsun Skyline that Maureen's husband drives. It's a small blue sedan with a white vinyl roof, well-kept and undented and trim. Plum has seen the vehicle countless times before: each time, it has meant nothing. Now, it's like a sty in her eye. She can't visit Maureen while the car is there. There's no reason why not, but she cannot.

Now and then, throughout the morning, Plum returns to her window to stare down into the garden next door. The lawn is a clean green rectangle, unoccupied. There's a flattened area where the picnic rug had lain. David's wading pool is still full of water—leaves fall into it during the afternoon, and scud about on the glinting surface territorially. The door of the Wilks house is shut tight against the gusting of the north wind. There's never any sign of Maureen. Plum puts her face to the pane, compresses her nose. "Some useful sister," she remarks. She bets her neighbor didn't bother to watch *Planet of the Apes.*

The difficulty of her homework stirs her temper after lunch, as does the unwieldiness of her books. She mumbles over her papers and pen until the grandfather clock, bonging in the hallway, provides an excuse for fury. "I hate that clock!" she screams downstairs; but her mother and father have gone to buy more clocks, and Cydar is wherever Cydar goes, and Justin is out in the driveway, hands on hips, considering the grizzled engine of his car. Plum stalks outside, where the breeze peppers grit against her calves and the scorched concrete makes her hop. Her brother does not look around, though he surely hears her approach. Near to him, she steps sideways onto a rockery, into the house's shadow. "Stupid hot concrete," she says.

"Stupid bare feet." Justin's own feet are shod with ancient black thongs which bear the impression of his toes. He's bare-chested, and wings of sunburned skin are peeling from his shoulder blades. The heat has stuck his dark curls to the back of his neck, his palms are grubby with grease.

"I'm bored," Plum tells him.

Justin bows deeper into the engine. Knuckles of spine show beneath his brown skin. "You can change the oil."

"I hate cars. I hate oil." She pokes her thumb through a hole in a monstera's leaf, and tears through the green platter to its edge. The noisy unzipping sound is satisfying; she chooses and cleaves another leaf. "Your car's a Holden," she states.

Justin says, "Hmm," under the bonnet.

"Is a Holden better than a Datsun Skyline?"

Justin's knees buckle under the atrocity of the question. Plum snuffles with amusement. She frees the monstera, slouches against the weatherboards. "But is a Datsun Skyline a good car, anyway?"

The vast steel bonnet is casting a blue shadow over Justin, so she cannot see his face well. "I guess it depends what you consider *good*. If you want to go and stop, not too fast, it's good. If you want to be ordinary and reliable and unadventurous, it's good."

Plum nods her head against the house. She can't decide what this information tells her.

Justin looks through the shadow at her, socket wrench in hand. "Why do you ask, Plum? Do you like the Skyline next door?"

"I'm not Plum anymore." The girl pushes abruptly away from the wall, steps into the white grip of the afternoon. "I've changed my name to Aria. Plum was a Skyline. You have to call me Aria."

On Sunday morning Mums stops in her daughter's doorway and says, "You're not coming to church, then?"

Plum is sitting up in bed, eating breakfast. She has already seen that the Datsun is still parked in the driveway next door, and the car has come to represent every false promise that's ever been made. She looks up sourly at her mother, her face still fuggy from sleeping, her hair an angry brawl. "I told you, I don't believe in God. God doesn't *exist*, Mums. I'm not going to visit somebody who doesn't even exist."

Mums holds an impervious silence. Her gaze roves the citadel of Plum's room, across the posters of cats and the dinky soft toys, over the clothes on the floor and the papers on the desk, along the cast iron of the bedhead. She is dressed in a lilac suit whose collar is crimped like a hibiscus flower — the color and style are in fashion, but Plum thinks, *Dowdy*. Like the house they live in and the objects with which they surround themselves, Plum's parents are old—both of them are over fifty, which makes them the most elderly parents she knows. A fact of which Plum is not proud. Their age makes it obvious to everyone who meets the Coyle family that Plum was a mistake which occurred when Mums and Fa were old enough to have known better, and should have been doing better things. "Anyway," Plum adds, "you can go to church without me. You don't need me there. You'll probably like it more. You can drive as slowly as you like. You can listen to your boring radio on the way. You can sing the hymns at the top of your voice. And after Mass you can yack for as long as you like. You only go to church to see your friends, anyway. You don't go to pray. I don't even reckon you believe in God."

Mums replies, "I'm disappointed, Plummy."

"Disappointed!" A bead of toast flies from Plum's mouth and lodges somewhere in the sheets. "*I'm* the one who should be disappointed! Why don't you ever just— *respect* me? *Respect* what I decide?"

To which Mums answers, "Why don't *you* respect *me?*"

Plum gapes, stunned by the lowness of this. "I'm not going," she growls. "I've decided. I'm never going to church again, so don't bother asking me. And don't call me Plum, either. That's not my name anymore."

"No? What do you want to be called?"

The ongoing presence of the Datsun has dissipated Plum's desire to please Maureen Wilks: but it is as if she is hitched to a terrible train whose track lies across everything that's brought happiness in the past. "Aria. *Not* Ariella. Aria."

"Aria." Mums's face crinkles around the word. "It's all right. A bit cold, I think."

"Cold? Cold!" A crust of toast leaps off the plate. "What do *you* care if it's cold? You never call me *darling,* or *sweetie,* or anything like that—*you're* the cold one, not me!"

"Plum!" calls Fa from downstairs. "Stop yelling!"

Mums retreats under the barrage. "Aria," she says. "I'll try to remember. But you might always be Plum Pudding to me."

She strides away in her churchgoing shoes while her daughter is rendered mute.

At lunchtime the next day, the topic is the new art teacher. The previous year, when Plum and her friends had been the babies of the school, the girls had accepted all facets of secondary-college life with awe and quiet dismay. Now, in their second year, their inexperience buffed from them, their place at the bottom of the hierarchy passed to a new influx of waifs, they are confident enough to complain about every aspect of the timetable, curriculum, faculty and uniform that doesn't completely suit them. The new year has brought to their academic lives many changes for the worse, including double periods of mathematics, detention for anyone who doesn't wear her tracksuit to gym, and a rearrangement of students into different homerooms, a move that has fragmented cliques and separated best friends. The art teacher is not the worst of the year's changes, but she is one of the more satisfying. There are so many offensive elements to the woman that it's hard to know where the annihilation should begin. "What about her dress?" Samantha's roaring. "It was foul! Like she'd spewed!"

"I thought I was going to chuck just looking at it!"

"It wasn't any worse than her face," says Dash.

"Her head's all pinched, like it was slammed in a book. . . ."

"And what does she call herself? *Mess?* Is that how you say it?"

"Miz," corrects Rachael. *"Not Miss, girls — Miz."*

"She went crazy when I said *Miss,* didn't she?" Which Sophie had done with her usual innocence that is easily misconstrued as stubbornness. *"Miz! Miz! Say it, girl! It's not difficult!"*

The friends, sprawled in the safety of their gang of seven, laugh like squeaky toys. It is another hot day, and they are gathered on the grass beneath their oak tree, sleeves pushed up to their shoulders, socks rolled down their shins. Last year they had all been in the same classes, but this closeness has been fractured by the new timetable: so the oak has become their assembling point at the beginning of each lunchtime and recess, the place to which they bring the gossip that has budded in their various classrooms. Here they talk to each other about pen-friends and enemies, siblings and parents, the superiority of T-bars over lace-ups. The seven of them are not among the most studious, most spoiled, most flirtatious or wealthiest of the girls in their year, but nor are they the most despised. They are the girls who lose library books, pass notes in class, audition for the chorus in the annual musical, plead weak stomachs when the time comes to dissect rats. Their stake around the shady oak is something better than they have earned, and one day the territory will be seized by an older, stronger, more justifiable gang—Plum is fatalistically sure.

"I don't care what she looks like, or what she wears." Rachael is lying on her back in the grass, keeping her pale self in the shade. The sight of the blue veins under the milky skin gives Plum the shudders. "The worst thing about her is she's trying to be our friend."

"Yeah! *Call me Miz, or call me Leah.*"

"No, not Leah: *Leearr.*"

"Yeah, *Leearr. Miz Leearr.* Talk to me, girls: I'm your *friend.*"

"Having a lady as a friend is OK," suggests Plum.

"Not if she's a *teacher!*"

"No, not a teacher," Plum agrees.

Victoria, fanning her face with a geography test, says, "Maybe if we refuse to call her Miz, she'll quit and leave?"

None of the others think this likely, so no one bothers to reply. The art teacher had offended Plum, not least when she'd grabbed her wrist and forced her to draw long lines over her crabbed daubings, chanting, "Loose movements, free, free!"—but a teacher is something about which nothing can be done, and there are other concerns on Plum's mind. For a start, she hasn't eaten. She had dropped her lunch—a chickenloaf sandwich and a pair of Kingstons parceled inside a creased chemist's bag—into a bin as soon as she'd arrived at school. It had proved an unexpectedly traumatic thing to do. Plum had projected herself forward, to this lunchless lunchtime; she'd looked guiltily back, seen Mums carefully slicing and bundling the bread. Nevertheless, swallowing hard, Plum had done what was needed. She's determined to whittle from her bones every dollop of fat that's blighting her life. And now, if not exactly ravenous, she is distressed by the sights and smells of lunchtime, by the baby-bird emptiness of her mouth. She has her drink bottle—Mums had put it into the freezer overnight, and the morning spent in Plum's locker has melted the green cordial into tactile shards—and she sips a few drops at a time. None of her friends have noticed she's not eating, but she runs interference over the grief this negligence is causing. "Hey," she says. "Guess what?"

Her friends look at her incuriously; Samantha rolls onto her stomach to tan her calves. "I'm changing my name," says Plum.

Dash peers flintily over the edge of her sandwich. She is tiny and smart in a way Plum will never be, like a small wicked dog on a leash. "To what?"

And it's only in this instant that Plum understands the courage the next moment will require. And that although she has no courage, it's too late for cowardice. "To Aria. Aria—like a song."

"Aaariaaa!" Caroline sings it, flinging back her heron head and thumping it into the oak. She clutches her skull, groans, "Ow ow": Plum thinks, *Serves you right.* In her truest thoughts Plum knows that she, Plum, is only tolerated amid these friends; and yet they seem to love Caroline, who in Plum's secret opinion is an absolute idiot. Who hasn't a brain to be damaged in her skull, who looks like a child kept in a cupboard for years.

"Aria is pretty." Victoria is blue-eyed and mellow, pink like a doll. "I wish my name was a song."

Samantha makes a spitting, guffawing noise, sitting up to yawn leoninely. As burly as a youth, no one wants to tell Samantha that she has translucent hairs along her jaw which glimmer in afternoon light. Her father travels, and every day since school resumed she has found reason to mention the fact that he has tickets to the opening ceremony of the Moscow Olympics. Samantha is a passer-of-notes, a whisperer-in-corners, a giggler-behind-hands, an exchanger of meaningful looks, the kind of person who should by rights be ostracized and spurned: yet it's Samantha whom they all battle to impress, Plum achingly included. If she could make Samantha *want* to be her friend, things would be almost perfect. "God, it's so *hot*." The strappy girl sighs expiringly. "What do you want to change your name for? Plum suits you. It's sort of . . . squashy."

"And juicy." Sophie doesn't mean it nastily; she is Plum's

original best friend. In the early days of their first year here, when they were both lost souls, she and Sophie had found one another, and made each other laugh. For a few months it had been just the two of them, sitting together on a bench eating lunch, saving chairs for one another in class, sleeping the night on each other's bedroom floor, and Plum had been happy. But then Sophie's charm had caught the attention of these others, and they had abducted her; Plum had been accepted as part of the deal, like Spam in a raffle-won hamper. The theft of Sophie had been traumatic, but not unexpected: as a kid in primary school, Plum had endured the abandonment of first one best friend and then, agonizingly, of another, and the reason for the phenomenon seems to be that there are flaws in Plum which become obvious over time, and render her companionship dissatisfying. The single positive aspect of Sophie's loss is that, diluted among the gang of girls, these flaws might not be so easily discovered. And it's not that Plum hates her friends, or that they completely hate her. Sometimes she loves them so much that her affection gives her pain. Yet she often wishes that Sophie had resisted them, and chosen to stay with just her. Life would be less . . . straining.

"And sticky," adds Dash.

"And stony-hearted." Rachael is their leader, one of the cleverest girls at school.

Caroline, still rubbing her head, comes to the rescue. "And sweet. That's why Plum suits you: because you're sweet. Don't be Aria, Plum."

"We don't like Aria," the others agree.

"But Plum is dumb! I should change it to something—more stylish. I met somebody who knows about modeling, and she said I could do it—fashion modeling. She said I have the hair and the face and the bones that magazines want . . ."

She trails off, realizing too late that she's peeled herself of skin. Under the navy shade of the oak tree her friends stare in post-nuclear silence. Scattered across the lawn are young ladies in paste-colored uniforms chatting, walking, squealing, luxuriating, smoothing Reef Tan into thighs. There are teachers wandering about on yard duty, pointing out rubbish that must go in a bin. There are leaves blowing about, chip packets scooting across the quadrangle, trucks changing gear beyond the gates. There is the school dog, Ebenezer, an overweight Labrador housed at the adjoining convent, rambling from lunch box to lunch box. From the tuckshop in the undercroft comes the summery scent of jam doughnuts, chocolate milk, damp salad rolls. Soon a bell will ring, summoning everyone back to class, where the teachers will drone exhaustedly and wilted discussions will take place, and the clocks above the blackboards will be watched with gamblers' intensity. It is Monday afternoon. It is the start of March. The week, the year, the whole torturous span of Plum's education stretches ahead of her. She doesn't know why she insists on making unbearable for herself this place that is already so hard.

Then they explode. "Hair like a wig?"

"A face like a cat's bum?"

"Everyone's got bones! What's so good about your bones? Even a dog wouldn't want *your* bones!"

"Hello, I'm Mizz Aaariaaa Coyle, I model cats' bums—"

"I'd like to thank my art teacher, Mizz Leeahh, for making me look like the Moaning Lisa—"

And even Plum is chuckling, as she absolutely must. Not being wounded by any of it, as she absolutely must not. "I'm just saying what she said!"

"Are you sure she wasn't blind?"

"What sort of fashion will you model? Paper bags for heads?"

Even lovely Victoria has never had the gall to suggest she could be in magazines: Plum sees in the eyes of her friends something hotter and more drying than the wind. With the exception of Rachael, who's calmly determined to study law, none of the girls know what they want to do with their lives. They foresee husbands and babies for themselves and each other, but there's emptiness surrounding these. Certainly there's nothing enviable awaiting Plum Coyle. "I think she was joking, Plum." Dash balls the plastic wrapper of her sandwich and throws it into the grass. "I mean Aria."

"Probably," agrees Plum, brutalized.

"It was a good joke, too," says Samantha; and the subject is forever finished with this final sword, leaving Plum to sag bonelessly. She sits plucking grass and smiling, listening to her friends talk. They talk about the Youth Group that has started in a scout hall near Rachael's home; Rachael and

Dash attended on Saturday night, and there's a boy—a man—the group leader, who must be discussed. "He kept looking at us," says Rachael. "He was looking, wasn't he, Dash?" Samantha glowers, "Why didn't you invite me?" and Dash has to placate her: "It was a spur-of-the-moment thing, Sam. You should come next week." But for the occasional snicker, Plum stays quiet. Her hands feel swollen, her eyes unwilling to blink. Lunchtime is never long enough, except for the days when it is too, too long, and this is such a day. Compared to sitting here, famished and steeped in shame, a classroom would be sanctuary.

But before the bell rings, which it must eventually do, Plum moves to repair her shaken standing. The bell will separate the gang into segments, and it's vital that these needle-pointed fragments go away well-disposed toward her. She drags out her voice like a grimy cloth, interrupts Victoria's assessment of her new headband to say, "I'm thinking of having a slumber party for my birthday. Should I?"

It's an important tradition of the group's, the remembering and fussing-over of one another's birthdays. In this, at least, Plum is an equal. "Hooray!" Caroline claps her hands. "I got a new sleeping bag for Christmas."

Rachael's slinky orange gaze fixes on Plum. "I know what to get you for your birthday, Aria. You'll love it. Dash and Sam, we'll have to pool our money."

Samantha looks at Plum for the first time. "Will your brothers be there? I'm only going if your brothers will be there."

"My brothers?" Plum frowns. "What? Why?"

"We like them, that's why."

"Yeah, we like your brothers."

"What do you mean?" Plum is confused. Her friends and her brothers have crossed paths on occasions when Plum has had one of the girls to the house—but she can't remember anything important ever being said. Her brothers, Plum knows, can never distinguish which of her friends is which. Justin is twenty-four, Cydar twenty-two: to them, Plum's friends are inconsequential, mere kids. Children to be tolerated for the sake of their sister; little girls to be otherwise forgotten.

But Victoria is saying, "Justin is the *biggest* spunk," and Plum can't believe her ears.

"Yeah, Justin's nice, but Cydar is better. He's got those black eyes—"

"No, Cydar's too scary! And Justin's got that voice and that smile—"

"But Cydar's . . . interesting. He hardly ever talks."

"They're both spunks," decides Victoria, and Caroline echoes, "Yeah, they're both spunks."

Dash looks at Plum. "So will they?"

Plum can only gape. Inside her mind are tussling demons. It's appalling to realize that her friends discuss her brothers behind her back—these friends who have just ground Plum herself under heel, and who don't have any decent brothers whom Plum might likewise admire. Justin and Cydar belong to *her*, and they are the best things

Plum has—her face flushes with possessive anger. Yet, at the same time, she sees that this turn of events is a gift. At primary school, some kids had trampolines or swimming pools; Plum had nothing, not even those pencils that could be sharpened by pulling a string. Now, suddenly, just when it counts, she has Justin and Cydar. A gift she can use, like ice picks on a glacier.

Dash says again, "So will they?"

Plum murmurs, "I'll ask them."

"Don't *ask*—tell them! You're their sister. They *have* to be at your party."

"Yeah—if they aren't coming, we won't be."

"Sammy!" scolds Sophie. "Don't say that!"

Samantha shrugs. "Joshing. But still."

"Yeah, but still," says Dash.

And Plum understands *but still,* two words as rough as rubble. Nevertheless she tries not to sound terrorized when she vows, "Of course my brothers will be there. Why wouldn't they? I'm their sister."

The bell clangs suddenly, a bomb that has been flying toward them in deathly silence for a long while. Across the green lawn girls stand and stretch. Plum and her friends gather their rubbish, tighten ponytails and adjust socks, sweep palms down the backs of their dresses. "Don't worry, Plummy," Caroline says, as they drift in the direction of the classrooms and the end of the sweltering day. "I'll come to your party, even if your brothers don't. I can bring my new sleeping bag."

☙ THE BUS RIDE TO AND FROM SCHOOL is a physics experiment for Plum. Each morning, pressed to the vehicle's seat, nose hovering close to the window on which there are smudges and sometimes a hair, a bubble inside Plum is pulled further and further into her depths until, as the bus draws up outside the school, it lodges in a quaggy place from which it cannot sink any deeper.

All day the bubble waits in the pit of her.

But on the bus ride home, the bubble rises. The journey is frustratingly stop-start, the vehicle crowded and noisy, the boys from the state school are medieval with sweat, there's no place on Earth less agreeable — yet still the bubble rises, a pearly bead inside a bottle of champagne. When Plum alights from the vehicle at the end of her street, her step is rarely jaunty, her mood not necessarily good; but she is a different person from the one she's been all day. Before she's flung back the screen door and announced, "I'm home!," the bubble has surfaced and shimmers opaquely, having returned to the light all her coarse clinging power, and all her love for those who must feel it.

She yanks the lid off the biscuit tin, sensing already the black fury that will rampage if all the biscuits have been eaten — fortunately there are four Iced VoVos at the rear of the tatty pack. She balances three in a tower on her hand, shoves the fourth into her mouth. "Mums!" she yells, slumping after her voice through the house. "Where are you?"

Her mother is in the laundry, picking through a pile of clothes still stiff from the line. She is sorting Justin's color-ful socks from Cydar's monastically dark ones. Plum halts in the doorway: "Is Justin home? Is Cydar?"

Mums holds up a sock to the light. "Justin's at work. Cydar's at university. They said they'd be home before din-ner. Is this sock black?"

"No, blue. You need glasses."

"Does Cydar wear navy socks?"

"Mums! Don't ask me!" Plum lurches away from the wall, collapses against the ironing board. "It's hot — it's so hot! Why is it so hot?"

"It's the weather."

"Weather! I hate weather. Can I have some money for party invitations?"

"Please."

"Please." Heavy as a washing machine turning its load.

"In my purse."

"What's for dinner?"

"Lamb fritters," says her mother.

"I hope there's tomato sauce," Plum warns. "I can't eat fritters without tomato sauce."

"There is sauce," Mums confirms.

Pausing only to pluck notes from her mother's purse, Plum moves upstairs. Her big slope-ceilinged bedroom is the place she most wants, every afternoon, to see. Her schoolbag, hulking with homework, is booted sideways across the floor. She strides to the window, looks down into the neighboring driveway, and the Datsun Skyline is gone. Her heart misses several beats. She changes out of her uniform, back turned to the mirror; in shorts and T-shirt she crouches beside the bed, drawing from underneath it the leather briefcase. The silver latches pop open alertly, *chock chock.* Her grandfather owned this case, it's a very old thing, but the latches are still strong. The key, unfortunately, is gone. If she had the key, Plum would keep it on a chain around her neck. Perhaps with something strung alongside to guard it, a shark's tooth or a small piece of gold.

Inside the case, the objects lie buttressed in their beds of cotton wool. Plum sucks her fingers clean of marshmallow before selecting her favorite, the lamb. It's a quaint thing, solid and see-through, with tiny black dots rendering surprisingly expressive eyes. If it were broken, the pieces would fit into a matchbox coffin. Its loss would be terrible, not least because something so powerful would be difficult to replace: but replace it she would, eventually. Perhaps with a charm bracelet, one dangling a dolphin and a cracked loveheart and a book that actually opens . . . Plum frowns, pondering. Even if the lamb remains unbroken, which it will, because it comes under Plum's protection, there is still space in the briefcase for a charm bracelet. It could coil thornishly between the jade pendant and the Abba badge. In fact, now that Plum thinks on it, there's no reason why the collection should not grow as large as the briefcase allows, assuming she can find enough suitable objects. She's stopped going to church, she's changed her name: maybe the collection should likewise evolve. The idea fills her with a blur of excitement. She imagines the briefcase packed to bursting, glowing like lava or a UFO, emitting a humming tone.

She kisses the knickknack and returns it to its bedding. The shadow of her hand passes over the broken watch, the yo-yo, the coin. She closes her eyes and spends a moment projecting her will. "Lovely things, lovely things, I am near; see me, hear me, need me, do as I say." If she were in a movie, there would be a pentacle painted on the floor in blood or red paint, a creaky tome opened on a stone altar, and candles burning everywhere. In a movie, her words would cause a gale to blow, send ravens cawing into the sky. All this is lacking, but Plum closes the lid satisfied, and shunts the briefcase under her bed.

She has a bike she used to ride when she was younger: lately she feels ridiculous upon it and prefers to walk. Outside, the heat presses on her head like the muscular palm of a revivalist. She lingers at the end of the fence, where the weedy corner of Coyle lawn meets the manicured edge of the Wilks'. *Bernie:* that's the name of Mr. Wilks, the man who drives the Datsun — she couldn't remember it before. The kind of man who says, "Another week gone," when you meet him putting out the rubbish bins. Plum hangs against the fence, picking at timber splinters. She could knock on Maureen's door, maybe get some party leftovers; she could tell her neighbor about the lunchtime conversation between herself and her friends. "They laughed at me," she would say, "because of what you said. You promised you'd be my friend, but then I never saw you, your door was closed to me." The thought makes Plum push away from the fence — she is, as always, forsaken. She is like the poor bird who is stoned to death in *A Girl Named Sooner,* which was a made-for-TV movie, but really good anyway. She crosses the road in depressed wandering steps; then remembers, on the footpath opposite, that she is superior, that suffering makes her strong. The cult leader's hand pushes hard on her head, but Plum ignores it. The heat is mighty, but she is mighty too.

The suburb in which she lives is muted and leafy, tall-treed and tile-roofed. Many of its residents have survived well beyond their necessity. Although the neighborhood is her home just as her bones are her own, Plum has never learned the street names, nor the names of the gardeners she sees in flower beds, nor the names of the flowers. Once in a bluish moon, an ambulance pulls up outside one of the houses; generally, however, the neighborhood is a place of nonevent. The loudest noise comes from mynas chastising cats, and from motor-mowers. Nothing happens, there is nothing to do, but Plum has hardly realized that yet. So far, it has been enough.

The neighborhood is served by a cluster of shops that line one side of an almost-busy road. Journeying, Plum traverses a cricket field where cricket is never played. The park hasn't been mown for some weeks, and pink daisies dot the grass. It's only when she is halfway across the oval that she remembers being stung by a bee while crossing this same grass wearing these same sandals one afternoon last summer. The bee, trapped between instep and sandal sole, had writhed in frenzy while Plum, screaming, had scrabbled in the grass like a broken-backed mule. The recollection makes her scan the daisies tensely, driving from her mind her usual park-induced thought, which is that she wishes she had a dog—a floppy cocker spaniel, or a bony Afghan hound. At home and at school she forgets the idea, as she would probably forget the dog. She is not really a nurturing person.

She arrives at the shops sweating, the preacher's hand on her head very tight and crawly, a hand which commits unpleasant sins. The shopping strip consists of a milk bar, a fish-and-chippery, an accountant's, and a hairdresser who deals with hair as an abattoir deals with life; as well as a news agency, which Plum enters. She wanders the length of the greeting-card rack until she reaches the party invitations. A poor or a daggy person might make her own invitations, but Plum is neither of these, so she needn't go to that trouble. After some indecision, she selects the dancing silhouettes of *There's going to be a party!* over the cavorting cavies of *Party's happening!* There are twelve cards in the box, so she will be able to make mistakes and give a spare to herself, as a joke.

Her fourteenth birthday. Her fifteenth year. Invitations that suggest youthful maturity combined with fun. Plum is happy. She spends her mother's change on a bag of Pop Rocks.

Paranoid about bees, she takes the longer route home, keeping to the footpath that skirts the oval. The path meets a playground where there are swings and monkey bars and a slide, all these constructed from chain and steel and hefty slabs of wood, as if children have the destructive strength of draft horses. Plum dallies on a swing for a while, kicking back and forth. She imagines that she presents a thoughtful picture to any onlooker. She climbs the ladder to the top of the slide and sweeps down the slant of steel; at the bottom of the slide she leaps off yiking, clutching the backs of her thighs. "Uh uh uh!" she cries, skittering forward but bending backward, away from the pain. As the agony subsides

Plum whips in circles, trying to see if her skin is cooked or perhaps flayed. She hisses at the slide, snatches the invitations from the grass, and thumps off grouchily.

Detouring along the footpath has led her away from her usual route; but there's another road, close to the playground, which will also wend her home. Plum stumps along, the invitations knocking her knee, impatient with the heat and wishing only to be home now, for the day to be done. She rounds a corner and sees, parked in the shade of a paperbark, a large, greenish, flat-flanked car so similar to Justin's that the word jumps out of her—"Justin!"—and she halts as if lassoed. Plum doesn't know Justin's plate number—she senses indistinctly the thousands of details she ignores every day—but the vehicle's familiarity, its relationship to her, is recognized in her marrow. She steps across the naturestrip, wary of bees, and peeks through the passenger window. There, on the long vinyl seat, is a scraggy striped fisherman's cap that is indisputably Justin's. There are his bronze sunglasses, folded on the dashboard. There, on the floor behind the driver's seat, is the street directory that Plum herself gave him for Christmas; it doesn't look like it's been used.

Plum crunches a mouthful of Pop Rocks, puzzling. Mums had said Justin was at work, but the bottle shop is nowhere near here. She looks around at the house before which the Holden is parked, thinking perhaps her brother is visiting someone; but the house is clearly owned by a geriatric, there are roses along the fence and a revolting gnome by the letter box, and no one young has lived there for decades. She could mull over the matter further, but it's easier to lean against the blank wall of cluelessness. "A mystery," she says, knowing it won't actually be so. The reason why Justin's car is here will not be astounding, due to the fact that so few things ever are. Plum walks away dispirited by the very dullness of existence.

Cydar is home when she arrives, and his presence revives her. She pushes through the jungly garden to where his bungalow, a large wooden cell as morose as a hangman, stands decaying in a corner of the yard. He is sitting on the bungalow's doorstep, a slinky black-and-white cat smoking a cigarette which he ashes with a tap against the step. The breeze wafts flakes of ash across his feet, and he watches them skip his fine toes and flat nails with a concentration that fades when he looks up at her. Sometimes, when Plum thinks of Cydar, she sees a mobile of origami cranes turning gently near the ceiling of a tall white ornate house like the one in *The Amityville Horror*. She has never told Cydar about this vision, because doing so would be as bad as shouting something that desperately needed to be kept secret. Cydar is clever, capable of demolishing his sister and everyone else with a tilt of his head, a lancet-like word — but he needs care. Plum doesn't know why, but she's always felt this way.

She flops on the earth beside his feet, hoping to appear winsome. Somebody, possibly the vampiric girlfriend, has painted his toenails blue. His eyes are very black eyes, and typically their whites are very white; today, the whites are stained scarlet, as if he's excruciatingly tired. She needs his promise immediately, however—she can't wait until he's slept. "So you're coming to my party?" she suggests wheedlingly.

He blows out smoke, blinks lacklusterly. "I thought I wasn't invited."

"I was *joking*. It was a joke! Of course you can come. So will you?"

"No."

"Cydar! You *have* to! I'm your baby sister!"

He concertinas the cigarette butt against the ground before flicking it into the shrubs, where it joins the slow perishing of stubs innumerable. "Yeah," he says. "That's the point."

"But you have to! *Please!* Pretty please? I'll write you a special invitation."

Cydar closes his eyes, pained. "Why would you want me at your party, Plum?"

"My name isn't Plum now. You have to call me Aria."

"All right. But I'm not coming to your party. All that shrieking."

"We don't shriek!"

"You're shrieking now."

Plum clenches her fists, struggling to find the right combination of words that will unlock his kindness. He will always do as she wants, provided she asks the right way. "What about if you just come for the cake?"

He thinks on this; then says, "All right."

Plum jounces with delight. She would seize her brother by his bony wrists and shake him to prove her gratitude, if only he wouldn't find the contact humiliating. Instead she inquires, "How's uni?"

She doesn't doubt that what her brother is doing at university will make a lasting impression on the world — she places no limits on his cleverness. But Cydar ignores the query, as if unconvinced that her curiosity is genuine. The trees rising above the bungalow scrape its corrugated roof with woody claws; from behind her brother's back comes the gurgle of a hundred aquatic worlds. The breeze has blown fine brown dust across his lips. For a moment she thinks he's forgotten her, that he's gone off wherever his fish go; then he looks at her and she's reminded that he never forgets anything. "What is it you want for your birthday? That thing you said you can't have?"

Plum pinkens, shrinking to recall the scene she'd made at the dinner table. There's no option but to brazen it out. "A television. A teeny-weeny television inside a silver ball with little legs. Like a spaceman's helmet. It's really cute."

"Sounds revolting."

"It's not! It's good. Just because it's not a dumb fish . . ."

"I thought you'd want your ears pierced."

Plum straightens with alacrity, hand flying to an earlobe. "What? Why? Do you think I should get my ears pierced?"

"No." Cydar shrugs. "All the girls wear earrings. I thought it's what you'd want."

Plum smooths the lobe between thumb and finger, dwelling on what piercing would mean. "I don't have to do what everyone else does," she murmurs.

"Nope."

"Maybe I should. Do you think I should?"

Her brother looks more tired than ever. "Everyone else does, so no."

This answer isn't satisfying; Plum, needing to think alone, climbs to her feet. "So you promise you'll come for cake?"

"I promise."

And she has to believe. Halfway across the garden she stops and looks back. He has rested his head on his knees, a hand on a foot, and looks like a crashed bird. "Where's Justin?" she asks through the tangle of briar and thoughtlessly planted trees. "Mums said he was at work, but I saw his car near the playground. Do you think he'll come for cake too?"

Cydar shrugs another time, and does not lift his head.

Into his knees, Cydar sighs. The hot breeze ruffles the hairs on his arms, rubs felinely against his face. The drug is moving oilishly through his system, making his limbs long like a spider's, loosening his skin. Grown in the black soil of mountains, fed by the crumblings of rainforests, watered by crystalline creeks and mothered by a radiant sun; transported interstate in Hessian bags in the wheel-space of a column-shift Valiant, a spotted dog's head poking out the window, the speedo watched religiously—all this journeying, from hard seed to sublime smoke, melts through time to peacefully unbuckle Cydar from normality. He had kept to himself the fact that, when Plum was sitting beside him, he could see her skull through her skin.

A rich, virescent, rank-smelling drug, strong as a train and loaded with paranoia: Justin, when he tries it, will be reduced to jabbering imbecility. Even Cydar, usually impervious, had had to fight the anxious urge to grip Plum by the collar and plead, *Don't: whatever you're doing, don't do it.* Cydar loves Plum and always has, from the moment he saw her on the day she was born. He remembers the hospital, standing beside Fa at the nursery window, pressing to the pane a card that said *Coyle;* he remembers the nurse walking the aisles of cribs until she came to one, their one, *his one.* Slotted inside her blankets, Plum was only a baby—only a baby's head, in fact, swollen as an apricot, spout-lipped, bald—but Cydar had craved to reach through the glass, *hello hello hello.* He had sought his father's eyes, and they had exchanged a look they've never shared since. Hushed and shivery. This new thing come to change everything. Make Cydar no longer the youngest, give Cydar something to guard. Plum loves Justin more than she loves Cydar, people usually do and cannot be blamed, and although he'd hoped that his sister might be something other than usual,

Cydar accepted the situation years ago. It's never diminished the rumble of responsibility he feels in his chest for her. But the honk of her voice, the slope to her stance, the sore look of the skin on her forehead, the unwillingness of her clothes to fit well: all these are making Cydar, who loves Plum more than anyone does, reluctant to look at her. The desperation which singes the edges of her — this is even worse. She's not fourteen, but sitting on the bungalow step Cydar is sure he sees how her life will unfold. *Be fearsome,* he wants to tell her. *Defy.* His own life depends on her doing so. His existence will never be all it can be if Plum stands in its corner, happy for and proud of him, but misaligned and alone. She will stunt him, and he will let her.

A blackbird breaks his concentration, the dope abruptly drops him from its teeth. Cydar yawns and straightens, rubbing his eyes with a fist. It's impossible to guess how much time has passed since he sat on the step and struck a match, but it must be nearing dinnertime. He stands up cautiously from the torpid trough of stonedness, and the chemicals sink through him to settle at his feet as heavily as boots.

The interior of the bungalow is lit like a cinema in which Gatsby would have watched silent films. The fish tanks emanate a frosty radiance that's shot through with amber and emerald. There is a damp, purgatorial smell. Standing against a wall are the handcrafted housings of an expensive hi-fi. Cydar flicks a switch, and threadlike needles jump. As the stylus arm rises, the record on the turntable begins to spin. Every day ends with The Velvet Underground.

There's not much time until lamb fritters, but enough to make a start on her homework. Plum takes the recorder and the book of tunes out to the swinging lounge on the veranda, and sits with the instrument perched on her lips and the book splayed over her knees. Plum is not musically inclined, and the noise she blows from the plastic tube is discordant in the extreme. *Like a cat trodden on by a plumber,* her music teacher says, having grimaced out the same line several hundred times over the past decade. Yet Plum persists, because she has in her head a seraphic image of herself playing a flute. She would be the exact person she wants to be, if only she could play the flute.

And Maureen, cooking dinner in her kitchen, might hear her playing, and come outside.

In fact, in the shadows, it is Plum's brother Justin who listens, unable, as long as his sister occupies the veranda, to step beyond the door.

MAUREEN SAYS, "Your sister asked if we were expecting a king."

Justin is standing by the window of Maureen's lounge room. The window is draped by a gauzy curtain, and while he can see out into a grainy world, no one, outside, may see in. Only stifled light penetrates the gauze — Maureen wants nothing to fade — so the room is dim, cool as a well even at the end of this long summer. Everything in the room matches — the smoked glass, the beige paintwork, the pair of Matisses framed in chrome — and accords with the current vogue of the middlingly classy. The lounge suite is upholstered in white leather, and reminds Justin of ice cream. The carpet is equally colorless, the enemy of shoes. It is a flawless but not a restful room: Justin has seen

Maureen's son refuse to cross the carpet-edger of its threshold, his deerish eyes blank with unwillingness.

Although right now the boy is sitting at Justin's feet tracing shapes with his fingertips onto the carpet, and Justin feels his presence as a whiff of Ovaltine and cinnamon toast.

The mantel clock strikes six with a ladylike chime. The clock is new, still foreign enough to make Justin and David look around at its sound. Maureen, stretched out on the ice cream, smiles: Justin knows why. She tends an ever-changing flock of costly periodicals, and every lounge room in their burnished pages features a small chiming clock on a mantel. Other things she sees there can make her less happy. "Yellow doesn't suit me, does it? But everyone seems to be wearing it. My skin's too pale for bright colors, isn't it? But colors are so much in fashion. Yellow is awful on me, I shouldn't have worn it."

"It's not awful," he assures her. "It's fine." Over the past year he's said this or something similar so often he hardly hears himself say it. In the beginning, he had thought her worries touching. It was as if she was trying to rise to a standard Justin had unintentionally set. Justin is twenty-four years old: the world will never be more suited to him than it is now, he will never feel more embraced by life or have greater faith in his right to exist. The earth and the oxygen, the cities and lights, the nights and the beaches seem created for him and for those like him. Maureen Wilks is thirty-six, married for most of that differing dozen years, a mother and a housewife. It would be tempting for someone like her, Justin supposes, to stop trying. Instead, in her relentless reaching for what's fresh and new, she's almost more youthful than he is.

But in the last few months something has changed, smudging his view of her. Something has leaked from a pool of indifference that Justin hadn't even noticed was filling, and everything he'd once craved has become less vital to him. The hankering he'd felt at the start is subsiding as it has subsided before, away from other girls he's loved, for no more scurrilous reason than that he's too restless to be in love for long. And although he's been aggrieved by the fickleness of his heart, Justin is also relieved. He is still free. He won't spend his life with this woman. He's embarrassed by the Justin who had once, boyishly, wanted to.

Embarrassment is like the fatal stick in KerPlunk — with the smallest tweak, everything falls. Justin now finds odious what once flattered and entranced. Maureen's conversation, her pride, even her attempts to please: all these irritate. Her battle to stay at the forefront of what's fashionable is pathetic in someone living her life. She doesn't seem willing to accept that she's just a middle-aged housewife. She speaks with dissatisfaction of the house, its furnishings, the neighborhood, the stores. And if she never exactly states that her husband and child also rank deficient in her world, she often tells Justin, "You are my fine thing. You're what's worth living for."

Such words had once sounded like poetry. Now they

slide off Justin forgettably. His immunity makes him pity her. To which Cydar had said: "That doesn't sound like love."

"I should have chosen the square face instead of the oval." She's referring to the clock, which is still trilling prettily, liking the sound of its own voice. Justin doesn't reply. If he's shanghaied into one more conversation about the price, prospects and quandaries posed by yet another piece of tat he will, without question, be sick.

David, overcome with weariness, stretches out on the carpet, resting his cheek on Justin's right shoe. A flame of affection lights up for the child, but Justin stamps it down. He leans closer to the window, searching out Plum. She's sitting on the Coyles' veranda, tooting a recorder. Through a scrum of camellia he glimpses her kicking foot, the back of a hand, the edge of her downturned face. If Justin were to leave through the front door, his sister would certainly spot him. Yet her presence isn't imprisoning—he could slip out the side door, jump the fence into the next property, walk from there to where he left his car. Plum would never see him, the buildings would block her view. Escape is not only possible, but easy, especially for one used to subterfuge—dressing for work he's not rostered to do, inventing the details of afternoons spent playing pool, learning another man's routine, memorizing the sound of a particular car. Never so much as a sidelong glance when there was a risk someone shrewd might see.

But instead of escaping, Justin simply stands, as if the

weight of the child's head has compressed his feet into the ground. He feels the exhaustion of doing what he hasn't yet attempted.

For a year they have played their game. A year of hands clamped to mouths, lipstick buffed from shoulders, care taken not to bruise. For much of that time, Justin's blood has run fast. Not so long ago, he would have loved Plum for sitting on the veranda and making an obstacle of herself. Now, though, he's bored. Now, he's longing for the freedom to leave through the front door. . . . The sight of his sister on the veranda swing is oddly beckoning. She must be waiting for Fa, or for Justin himself. And he wants to go and wait with her: if he could sit beside her, waiting for Fa, rightness would be restored. As long as he's here, behind a gauze curtain, nothing is as it could be.

Justin is not like Cydar, brilliant and tightly-wound. He is not clever in the way a successful man needs to be. He has bumped through life like a brightly colored ball—laughing, disorganized, freewheeling, easily pleased. Sweet-natured, he almost always meets sweetness in return; and is not hurt when he doesn't, but baffled and forgiving. Every aspect of his world has made Justin vibrantly happy. But the situation with Maureen has become the kind of darkness that's never shaded his existence before, and Justin has started to resent her for it. *Shut up*, he wants to tell her—he, who's never had to be cruel.

"A king." There's something of the dying swan in the crook of her neck, the mammoth surrounding of whiteness. "We had everything a birthday has to have—candles, cupcakes, fairy bread, the song. David really wanted you to be there. So did I, Justin."

"I know. But I told you I wouldn't be. I told you not to make an effort for me."

"I didn't make an effort for you. I made an effort for David. And we had Plum as a guest, which was nice."

Justin thinks on this. "Plum didn't tell me she came to the party."

Maureen lifts her chin. "Why should she?"

There's no short answer, so Justin says nothing; but distantly he realizes something that is difficult to put into words. If his sister becomes friends with Maureen, the darkness in Justin's life will spread.

Then Maureen smiles, and the unease falls from Justin as swiftly as it had flared. She is just a poor matchstick girl, lonely and trying to please. And he has loved her — known himself, at one time, to be hopelessly *in love* with her. And for a moment he's captured by what has always fascinated him: her willowy height, her knowingness, her tightly-drawn clothing. Even the fact that she has had a child is inexplicably compelling; even the fact that, most nights, she lies in somebody else's arms. He can't go back, can't revive what has died, but Justin is grateful for having known her. His life, when she's gone, will absorb the occurrence of her, and bounce on like a ball down a grassy green road: but for some time he will surely feel a loss, the emptiness of the hands of the smoker who finally renounces nicotine.

* * *

Maureen is, in fact, a closet smoker, sneaking a pack's worth of Alpines into her lungs each week. She smokes in secret for the sheer pleasure of secrecy. She smokes because, smoking, she is nineteen again, on the shore of possibilities.

These end-of-summer dusks never want to finish. The light lingers until it makes a nuisance of itself. David won't sleep if there's a chink of luminance behind his bedroom curtain. He asks for a story and then for another, until she tells him, "No!" He swallows the word like a swordfish, closes his eyes instantly.

Grayness lies along the fence and gutters; except for this burned periphery, the sky is mango-orange. Maureen is wearing a cream-colored dressing gown which scuds around her ankles; beneath the gown, a white silk slip grasps the curvings of her body. Mosquitoes come to dance attendance on her, lances at the ready. She breathes smoke at them and they shy sideways like knights. She wanders up and down the garden path, lingering at its far reaches, her weight hinged on a hip. Deep in the warm dirt, the crickets say nothing: it's so quiet that Maureen can hear the cigarette burn, hear the leaves slide against one another. Presumably the neighborhood is bedded down with *Reader's Digest,* careless of the jewel-like evening beyond the door. It is perfection; and Maureen feels perfect. Her body is washed, her hair squeakily clean. She sniffs the crook of her arm, where Justin had lain, but there's only the Nordic scent of the bath.

A light is shining in the girl's bedroom, the blind lifted

and the window open. Maureen knows this is a signal for her. She crushes the cigarette on a stone, slips the stub into her pocket. "Aria!"

Hardly an instant passes before the girl's face appears at the window, white and passionate. The blue pajamas she's wearing look stale as a serviette. "Maureen! I'll come down—"

"No, stay there. I've missed my Rapunzel."

"Did you remember to watch *Planet of the Apes?*"

"I did. Those vicious gorillas!"

"And what about the ending? Were you surprised?"

"I was surprised, and I thought it was sad. What about you, though? How have you been? How was school?"

"OK." The girl's face contorts. "I threw my lunch in the bin."

"Oh! Good girl!"

"And I told my friends what you said about me becoming a model. They all laughed at me."

Maureen pauses, hearing the blame. "And these friends of yours know a lot about fashion photography, do they?"

". . . No."

"Then of course they laughed. They're jealous."

It's evident that Plum hasn't thought of it like that. Her shaggy head, framed in the window, bobs avidly. Maureen says, "Don't listen to poisonous people, Aria. You don't need friends like that."

"No, I know. But—they're nice to me, most of the time."

She's worrying that Maureen will divine she's a lesser equal among her friends. So Maureen answers, "I'm sure they are. But don't forget, I'm here if you need me. And I will never laugh at you."

The girl ducks her head, says, "Can I ask something now?"

"Of course." Maureen glides nearer the fence.

"Do you think I should get my ears pierced?"

Maureen clasps her hands. "Why not? You'd look lovely."

"Lovely." Plum scoffs. Something in the distance catches her eye and makes her scowl. "Your—Mr. Wilks—is coming. I can see his car."

Maureen says, "Poor Bernie. He works late."

"I'm writing invitations!" The girl beams. "I chose the ones with silhouettes."

Maureen smiles up at her, though she has no idea what the girl means. She says, "Aria, would you be interested in babysitting David occasionally? Playing with him, taking him for walks? He likes you, and I want him to have friends. I'd pay you, of course. You could save to have your ears pierced."

The girl hesitates as the Datsun swings into the driveway and rushes up the concrete guides. Maureen hears the hand brake secured, the driver's neat door eased open. "I would, I will," Plum decides swiftly. "Maybe I'll see you tomorrow?"

* * *

Cydar pauses, stilled as a prowler hearing a lamp switched on. The door to Plum's bedroom is unlatched, and through the gap he sees a sliver of cupboard festooned with stickers and pictures cut from magazines. Only his sister's voice carries through the gap, but he guesses who she's talking to. When the window rumbles down its frame he uses the noise as a thief uses darkness, to proceed.

Justin is lying on his bed wearing a pair of Fa's old trousers and a set of headphones, each cup the size of a muffin. The room is dark, the blind is down, his arms are folded across his chest; Cydar thinks of an Irish farm boy laid out on the kitchen table. Seeing him, Justin pulls off the headphones and drops them to the floor, where they bark out tiny noises like furious miniature dogs. Cydar asks, "Why don't you turn on a light?"

Justin's glance goes to the window; Cydar looks wry. "You're a rat in a wall," he says.

"Yeah." Justin smiles, in Cydar's mind transforming from dead farm boy to dying matinee idol. "A rat in a wall."

Cydar takes from his pocket a snugly bound parcel of marijuana and tosses it onto the bed. The drug will wreak havoc on Justin and his laconic friends, but Cydar is nobody's keeper, and charity is a trait that, from childhood, he's understood to have its own rewards. He hesitates before stepping over the threshold — he doesn't often come into Justin's room, this attic-space of maleness and dog-eared car manuals, its walls hung with glum oil paintings that Justin didn't choose; but when he does, Cydar makes a beeline for the single curiosity. On the chest of drawers is a shallow bowl that has a rotating base. The interior of the bowl is divided into six compartments, each with its own flip-top lid. The lids are inscribed in copperplate: *cuff links, rubber bands, spare change; paper clips, safety pins, keys.* A manly ornament from two decades earlier that attracts Cydar like fireworks. He spins the bowl, the lids whirl around — then stops it sharply with a jabbing finger. *Paper clips.* Lifting the lid reveals not paper clips but a purple button entangled in cotton. Pleasing nonetheless, and Cydar smiles. Justin says, "Just have it. Take it."

"I don't want to."

"Well, I don't need it. I don't even know how it got here."

Cydar knows: Fa had brought the bowl home from a junk shop, and put it in Justin's room without even considering that his younger son might appreciate it more. But Cydar tells Justin, "If I take it, you'll have nothing. Nothing except that cat outside the wall."

Justin draws breath to reply, but doesn't; his chest falls, his fingers close around the crackly bag of dope. Cydar waits, spinning the bowl. Beneath them the house sighs, shifting wooden bones on its stumps. They feel the weight of the dust that coats the roof joists and sloughs from the plaster and lies between the floors; they feel the presence of their mother and father in the den downstairs, their sister moving in her bedroom down the hall. Cydar keeps his voice low, as if the house is one of cards. "I told you you'd regret it. I said you were an idiot."

Justin says, "You're not helping."

Safety pins. "Have you ever owned many safety pins?"

"You've asked me that before."

Cuff links, spare change, rubber bands. If the bowl is spun fast enough it makes a turbulent sound, and its wants become *cuff change, key links, spare paper bands.* "Plum was talking to her just now. Hanging out the window like Juliet."

"They're friends." Justin tucks the dope under his pillow, resumes the corpse position. "Plum went to David's party, and now she and Maureen are friends."

Cydar lifts his head, and across the dark room the brothers exchange the kind of glance that might have passed between brother gunslingers, or brother mobsters, or brother politicians. They understand one another's inconveniences; they are uncommonly reliable; they are faithfully in-league. "She saw your car in the street today. She thought it had broken down."

Justin says nothing immediately; under the bed, the minuscule dogs continue to bark. Cydar hears the squeak of the tape that's rolling in the machine. Kiss, *Dynasty,* Justin's playing it to death. "The situation is becoming complicated," he eventually acknowledges.

Cydar cannot help but be angered. "It's not for nothing they advise against shitting where you eat."

"Yet again," his brother sighs, "you're just not helping."

The bowl spins like chance, round and around. "Maybe it will be all right," Cydar suggests. "It might be good for Plum to have Maureen as a friend. Someone older. Smarter. I don't think Plum . . . does very well."

"It's a complication," Justin says shortly.

"Well, what are you going to do about it? Lie here and hope it goes away?"

"Will that work?"

Cydar's lip hooks; he halts the bowl with such suddenness that it tips. "Rubber bands."

"My least favorite."

"More useful than safety pins."

"Debatable," says Justin.

Cydar idles a moment longer before turning his back on the siren bowl. "Well, good luck with all that," he says, moving to the door. "You know where I am if you need me."

"Yeah," his brother answers. Sleeping with the fishes.

THE RUBBISH BINS weren't emptied overnight, and the dented metal drum contains a vile mess of orange peel, squashed banana, shattered crackers, snapped laces, balls of cling wrap, icy-pole paddles, torn foolscap, masticated chewy, sucked and spat-out sweets. Flies loop the inside of the bin like racing cars; there is the odor that is the universal companion of garbage, subterranean and punchy, innately unclean.

Plum stands beside the bin, lunch in hand. Today it is Strasbourg with sauce. If she breathed the sandwich deeply she might smell the kitchen at home, the blade of the knife, the scarred chopping board. She might smell Fa eating breakfast, Cydar smoothing the headlines, Justin asleep upstairs. More than anything she might find her mother's hand laying out the Strasbourg so it doesn't overlap the crust, tamping the bread lightly, cleaving the sandwich in two. Binding the meal in rainbow wrapper, pressing out the air so the bread will be soft when Plum eats it, with no gritty scalp of staleness.

She thinks of Maureen, who in the garden last night had looked like a white angel pacing a heavenly cemetery. Plum wants to be thin, but mostly she wants the angel to look at her with pride. Still, after she's laid the sandwich in the bin, she has to move away quickly, thinking sturdy thoughts. The assembly bell is ringing, so she has an excuse to run.

At recess she meets her friends underneath their tree. Something exciting has happened overnight: Rachael has seen the Youth Group leader walking on the street. "But what did he *do?*" Victoria urgently needs to know. "Did he remember you?" Of course the boy-man had remembered Rachael—he'd been staring at her throughout the entire Youth Group meeting just nights before. He hadn't stopped to talk on the street, he'd seemed busy, as if he was going somewhere—but he *had* smiled and said hello, and asked if Rachael would be at the next meeting. Plum listens avidly to this report, veering as they all are between excitement and jealousy. Apart from a childhood crush on one of Justin's friends, and a current, less sustainable besottedness with David Bowie, she has not yet encountered any men to really like. She's nervous at the prospect of what will happen when she does. She doesn't know how to kiss, nor trusts that she'll be able to do so when the moment comes. At home, there's a book about boys-meeting-girls, a book Mums bought for teenage Justin, who'd never needed advice. Plum has read it countless times, but every time she does she becomes a little less sure. How to get from meeting a boy to . . . *that*. . . . It's a relief to change the subject when Rachael's story peters away. "Invitations," Plum says, passing out white envelopes.

"Oooh, invitations!" A smear of chocolate spreads immediately from Caroline's fingers to the paper.

Dash pulls out the folded card and reads the words inside; then looks critically at the jiving silhouettes pictured on the cover. "Do we have to dance at this party?"

"You don't have to. There'll be music, but we can just listen." Dash's foxy face remains suspicious, so Plum adds, "I don't like dancing either."

"Aria!" Samantha is shocked. "How can you hate dancing? The only people who hate dancing are people who are hopeless at it."

"Well, I don't hate it—"

"You said you did!"

Plum fumbles, feeling she's slipping down a ladder. Already the day is too hot and long. "I don't like dancing in front of *good* dancers, I meant. It's better just to watch them—"

"*Watch* them? You better not sit around watching *me*. That's creepy, Aria."

Caroline has been counting on her fingers. "The party is three weeks away!"

Plum turns, agitated. "Two and a half weeks. That's all right, isn't it?"

"No! Two and a half weeks? I can't wait that long!"

The sweetness of this makes Plum blink, doused by a desire to hug this scrawny simpleton of a girl. A far-off idea occurs to her, to steal Caroline away from these others, to make it just the two of them. Such a life would be, Plum knows, undemanding. But the friends would never surrender Caroline, and Plum, in the next instant, isn't convinced she wants her. Life would become pointless so quickly.

Victoria swats at a fly with her card. "What about your brothers? Will they be there?"

"They said they will." Plum hesitates, then takes the risk. "They said they were looking forward to it."

Rachael frowns. "Why would they *look forward* to it?"

"That's creepy too," says Samantha.

"Ugh," Plum gags. "No, that's not what they said." *Why, why, why* must everything be a battle? "They said they'd be glad to see you again."

This is so wily that Plum is thunderstruck. Rachael actually colors around her collar. Samantha says caustically, "They would have meant *all* of us, not just you, Rachael. Not *everybody* you meet falls in love with you, you know."

"I *don't* think that," Rachael snarls; "Yes you *do*!" Samantha howls.

The two glare at each other; in the silence that falls, Plum races away with her advantage. "And guess what? I've decided to get my ears pierced."

It is something she's been thinking about all night, and she's resolved that it's the thing for her. But Caroline cringes: "It hurts, Plummy! I cried."

"You did cry! I remember."

"Yeah, I bawled. I almost peed my pants."

Plum shrugs, full of cardboard courage. "I have to save up the money first. I'm getting paid to babysit the kid next door. When I've saved enough, we can go to the chemist and get it done."

"You'd look good with gold studs, Plum."

"Do you think? I was thinking silver sleepers—"

"No," says Samantha, "Victoria's right. Studs would look better. Sleepers look best on skinny girls. Not saying you're fat, but you're not skinny-skinny, you know? And sleepers only suit skinny-skinny girls."

The bell rings, peeling out importantly from speakers around the grounds; Plum realizes with surprise that she's forgotten to eat her biscuits. The friends pick themselves out of the grass, dust off their dresses, hitch up their socks. As they stroll toward the buildings, Rachael has an idea. "*We* could pierce your ears, Aria. Then it wouldn't cost you anything."

Instantly they're eager. "Yeah! Yeah! We should!"

Plum slows, eyes rolling horsily. "Do it—how?"

"Easy! We numb your ear, then jab the needle through. Exactly like they do at the chemist."

"But the chemist uses that machine, it only takes one second—"

"Shut up, Caz. This is the same. Only a zillion times cheaper, so Aria won't have to babysit some screaming brat . . ."

Plum pauses in the doorway of the building, completely barren of words. Her friends gaze at her hopefully — only Samantha, that giantess, is taller than she is, and Plum feels stretched and unstable, as if hoisted on a wire. Then Sophie says, "We could do it at my house on Saturday. My parents are going to a wedding," and Plum's confusion drops away; she sees.

"Say yes, Aria!"

"It will be fun!"

Inside Plum there's a sonar whine of fear, but she's thinking, now, of the benefits — *happiness, power.* The pain will pass, but the benefits will remain; and the chance might never come again. "OK." Her voice is mossy. "Saturday. It will be fun."

"I'll bring the needle," says Samantha.

They push through the doors into the leadenness of the building, into chatter and banging metal, dropped books and chanting and shoes scuffing stone. Girls are singing, reciting, bouncing balls, bickering. The second bell starts to ring, warning students to look sharp. Lockers slam, stories end, panics are flown into. Plum, already terrified, madly thinks *happiness,* feveredly clings to *power.*

* * *

The glass lamb doesn't have an interesting story. It is not, for instance, something that Princess Anastasia Romanov kept on a shelf in her onion-domed bedroom alongside a clutch of Fabergé eggs. Rather, it was bought by a country girl on a rare jaunt to the fancy shops of the city. The girl and her mother had caught the train all the way from their property on the flat sheep plains. Journeying, the girl had counted her money. She did not know what she would buy — maybe a bangle or a hatpin. But when she saw the lamb in a jeweler's window, she knew what she couldn't live without. The girl grew up, married, had children; became, in time, a grandmother. The lamb remained with her throughout those years. No one was allowed to touch it, only to admire from afar. Then one day, in a fit of generosity regretted ever since, the grandmother gave the lamb to her favorite granddaughter, and has never laid eyes on it since.

The jade pendant is not the prettiest thing. It is a cheap souvenir from Hawaii. Like many souvenirs, it had seemed a good idea at the time. In the shop, surrounded by chips of lava and carvings of splay-faced deities, the pendant had stood out as comparatively beautiful. And while it does indeed have some grace, the hard green stone curving sinuously from the silver clasp and leather string, it is impossible to avoid noticing the rust on the silver, the scragginess of the string. It is nothing but a trinket for a tourist lacking taste. But it was her first and only holiday overseas, and she'd worn the necklace throughout the trip—swam with it, sunbaked with it, hiked a volcano while wearing it, so it slithered across her sternum slick with sweat—and it has value beyond its worth, because of these memories.

The yo-yo came from the Royal Show. Every year she waits patiently for the ten-day spectacular that is the Show. She studies the showbag guide as if somewhere within the roll-call of goodies is secreted the meaning of life. Each year she takes a day off school to arrive at the showgrounds as the gates open. The first hours are a rush, riding the Zipper before the great crowds arrive, visiting the exhibition halls to see which handmade quilt took out the prize. Only the last hour is devoted to showbags. She's decided in advance which are the best value. At home she spills the haul across her bed, burying her face in a sugar mountain. . . . The year she was eleven, the mountain was slightly smaller than usual. Passing a toy stand, she'd made a mature decision. She would eat the lollipops over the course of many days, but eventually they would be gone. If she bought a yo-yo—and although she's not skilled in the toy's use, she envies those who are—she would have something to keep. She chose the orange one advertising Fanta, which is her favorite drink.

The old coin is not as old as, for instance, a coin of Nero's or Henry VIII's. It is only a penny of the sort recollectable by anyone's parent. Yet it looks ancient—thick and stained and very brown, as if the years spent lying in the dry dust beneath a house rendered it as parched as a mummy. Circling its edge are words printed in perfect letters, and on one side there's a fast-flying kangaroo. The man in the coin shop said it has no value whatsoever; but it is worth something to her. It was found by her uncle on the day she was born—she doesn't know what he was doing under the house, but when his kneecap detected something inflexible and, investigating, he excavated a penny which, by coincidence, had been minted exactly fifty years earlier, it seemed as good a gift as any to present to his new niece. History in the shape of a disc. The first time she'd pressed it to her lips, she discovered the old metal was warm.

The Abba badge is, by comparison, youthful, and several times the size of the coin. She is not a musical girl nor, intrinsically, a joyful girl; but the music of the four Swedes shook something awake inside her, and when she heard it she felt airborne and strong. When she saw the handsome foursome on television she knew the longing of one reared among a foreign species encountering, for the first time, others in the image of itself. Every night, around the ages of nine and ten, she lay in bed pretending Frida was about to knock at the front door. They would all fly home to Sweden, where she would live in a luxurious log cabin. While waiting for this to occur, she painstakingly saved enough money to buy the badge, which she wore every weekend for months. Agnetha, Anni-Frid, Benny and Björn stood valiantly over her heart. It was the sort of love affair one grows out of, but she never threw the badge away. Even now, so much later, she occasionally thinks of Frida's knuckles on the door.

The watch has a tiny face barely larger than a fingernail. The face is encased in silver; the strap is a thin line of black leather, and the buckle is also silver. It was once a pretty accessory, given to the mother when the mother was eighteen, passed to the daughter when the daughter turned twelve. That had been a mistake. A stumble in the schoolyard resulted in a broken wrist and a broken wrist-strap as well. In the pain and mayhem, the watch lay on the bitumen, trampled to the point of being unfixable. The glass is crumpled, the silver scarred, the little hands are jammed. It's still a lovely thing, however, and receives grave nursing when she dares to touch it. Everyone thinks it disappeared forever in the broken-wrist chaos: but she still has it, and she's never shown it to anyone, because it and its injuries belong to her.

Plum can't explain exactly what all these treasures are meant to achieve, but together they work to give her something she can't achieve on her own. Happiness, safety, power, place—none of these words is precisely correct, but none is absolutely wrong either. In owning the objects, she isn't helpless; she could be, she fancies, almost lethal. She could be like Sissy Spacek in *Carrie*. Yet sometimes—often—the objects' influence weakens, leaving Plum to flounder. When it happens, Plum is teased and ignored. Perhaps she should intensify her time with the talismans — wear the badge, carry the coin, fling the yo-yo around. Sleep with them cuddled against her stomach. Maybe she should . . . eat them.

. . . No.

She kneels above the opened briefcase, radiating energy through her hands and into the objects; simultaneously she sucks up *their* energy, in a paranormal transference that would impress Doctor Who. "Make room," she tells the collection, her eyelids fluttering druggedly. "Prepare for the expanding of your supremacy. Prepare, prepare." And she does in fact feel a tingling in her palms, which could well be a manifestation of something that has nothing to do with the real world.

What's left of the week passes quickly, as if Saturday is a whirlpool sucking down the days. Plum is excited, and afraid. She wakes each morning with her heart running fast; at night she has stressful dreams. Even sitting in the dark beside Justin watching Wednesday's late movie, *Logan's Run,* doesn't distract her as it normally would; nor even does Michael York. Fortunately, her nervousness makes it easier to throw away her lunch. Plum has more important things to think about than her mother's wasted time.

Sitting cross-legged over her homework each night, licking ice cream from the back of a spoon, she listens for the sound of her neighbor's door stretching out its hinges. She knows that Maureen walks in the garden most evenings because of her love for the warm dusk air. But the Datsun Skyline arrives in the driveway some time during Wednesday night, and when Maureen appears in the garden on Thursday she is in the company of Mr. Wilks. The two of them sit on the lawn with glasses and red wine, and Maureen laughs loudly, warning Plum she's not alone. And it's true that Plum shies sulkily from the idea of sharing her friend, even with this unchallenging man. Her friendship with Maureen is like a white unicorn in a forest, or maybe a ruby in a cloud. It is very unusual and shiny and delicate. She would rather not speak to Maureen at all, than have someone overhear what she'd say.

Thankfully, on Friday evening Maureen is in the garden with David. Fit to burst, Plum runs down the stairs, across the lawn and up the neighboring driveway, her arms crashing at her sides. Maureen laughs to see her hot red face, her vibrant ready smile. She pats the grass, and Plum flops down. The girl is desperate to tell everything — every musing and emotion that has passed through her in fourteen years — and most particularly she wants to talk about what's planned for the following day. But Plum senses Maureen will not approve of the domestic ear-piercing — she will say it's a dangerous, unhealthy idea. If Plum explained that she is offering her ears to the administrations of her friends because it will make them happy and thus make Plum happier, Maureen would probably understand; but she would say Plum was being absurd. And it's impossible to tell even someone like Maureen about the treasures in the briefcase, which are giving her strength but which need to be stronger. So, "Hi, Davy," she chirrups. "Is that your new truck?"

The boy, in the sandpit, glances at the yellow dump truck. "I got it for my birthday."

"It's my birthday soon—"

"I know," the child drawls. "Mum told me."

"How is everything?" Maureen asks. "Tell me what you've been doing."

Plum slumps on her elbows, the grass tickly on her skin. "Nothing's been happening. Everything's the same. I watched *Logan's Run*. It's a science-fiction movie where everyone has to die when they turn thirty. But thirty is pretty old, so I don't know why they complain."

"It's not so old," says Maureen.

"It's not *old*." Plum hurries to make amends. She doesn't know exactly how old Maureen is, but she must be fairly old to be married with a house and a son. "It's just—old *enough*. People shouldn't try to cling on to everything—"

"Even to life? To pleasure?"

This is not what Plum wishes to talk about; her fondness for *Logan's Run* is diminishing. "I haven't been eating my lunch," she says instead. "I'm used to it now, I hardly even get hungry. I gave out my party invitations, and everyone can come. . . . My friends want my brothers to be at the party. I think they want Cydar and Justin there more than they want me."

"I doubt that's true, Aria."

"They said they wouldn't come unless Justin and Cydar were going."

"Well, that's just girls being silly."

Plum nods wonkily, startled by the dismissive truth of it: what seems imperiling is really just girls being silly. It is miraculous, how easily Maureen makes dire things laughable. "My friends are mean to me sometimes," she says. "I don't know what to do."

Maureen is running her fingers down the length of her arm. She doesn't say it's better to have no friends than to have horrible friends. She says, "Use their nastiness to make yourself stronger."

Plum feels a strange eeriness. The objects seem to call out like a choir from the briefcase. "What do you mean?"

"You know what I mean. You have a whole life to get through, Aria. A lot longer than thirty years, probably. Don't waste it being weak and easily hurt."

Plum's breath hitches: Maureen would understand about the ear-piercing and the briefcase. There are no limits to what Maureen will understand. She opens her mouth to explain, but the words simply won't budge. The risk is too great: Plum could not bear it if Maureen lost her liking for her. She swallows the surge of confessional honesty, her damp gaze careering. In the window of her bedroom are reflected the branches of the melaleuca where the little owl lives — Plum has listened and listened futilely for its hoots. Further along is Justin's window, closed tight, blind down.

The roof of the house is scaled with lichen; the sky beyond is purple, as if it's suffered a horizon's-worth of blows. There are no birds, but there are midges bouncing on the air, and underground a cricket is tuning its saws and pins. She looks back to Maureen and asks, "Will you come to my party? Even for a little while?"

Maureen smiles. "Aria. Of course I will."

And Plum grins bashfully, hugs her knees to her chest. Warmth fills her stomach when she imagines the scene: her elegant neighbor making her friends feel ugly, her admirable brothers reducing them to giggling fools. *Yes,* she will say to Rachael and Samantha and Dash. *This is my actual life. This is ordinary for me.*

Things will be different after that.

David is heaping sand into the tray of the dump truck, making a truck's growling noise. Maureen has tipped her face to the sky and closed her black-panther eyes. A midge has landed and is walking on the fine skin of her neck. "What an evening," she breathes. "Hardly a cloud. Shh, David, don't make that noise."

Plum glances at the sky—no stars are out yet, and the moon is as cracked and colorless as a cafeteria plate—but her eyes, compelled, flick back to the midge. Maureen's hands rest in her lap, she doesn't seem to feel the insect's exploration. "Summer is leaving us again," she says. "Nights like this always make me sorrowful."

"Sorrowful?" Plum's voice is a donkey's bray against a cheetah's sigh. "How come?"

"Because it feels like something lovely is ending, and all that's coming is coldness."

The girl stares at the woman, whose closed eyes and unmoving body are like moats. A bird cries in the she-oak and the cricket stops creaking: in the garden's sudden silence David's hands grow still, he turns his face away. "Daddy," he asks distractedly. Plum, embarrassed, dredges something to say. "It's sad when good things finish. I don't like change. I don't care if bad things finish. But good things shouldn't change."

"Aria. A moment ago you said that people shouldn't cling to things."

Her immediate instinct is to twist and weave, attempting to justify her nonsensical self. To anyone else in the world, she'd do it. But there's relief in conceding to Maureen, "Yeah. I get confused sometimes. Real life isn't the same as a movie."

"No, it isn't. Everything has to change, Aria. There would be something very bad about a good thing that didn't change."

"Where's Daddy?" David asks loudly. Plum and Maureen ignore him. "Like robots," Plum offers, trying hard.

"Exactly." Maureen's eyes go to the girl. "Human beings change. Who you are now is not the person you'll be in a few years. The things you do, the decisions you make — they won't always seem right, later on."

Plum nods; she accepts this is true for some people, but not necessarily for herself. She is, after all, already quite astute. Rather than point this out, she says, "There's a crea-ture on your neck. An insect. A gnat."

Maureen's hand rises to her throat. "Aria, I almost forgot. Would you babysit David on Sunday? I need the afternoon."

Plum has no choice but to say, "I guess."

"I'll pay you, of course." She smiles quickly at Plum, who smiles back instantly, adjusting her features to cov-etous. But Maureen's searching fingers have crushed the midge into a paste, and the sight of the mess on the grace-ful throat is disturbing and somehow disappointing. Plum had imagined Maureen was above such helpless, human things.

The following day dawns clear. Plum wakes earlier than usual, a tall solid girl lying haphazardly across a bed, her blue pajamas pinched in the brown clefts of her body. She lies, humming dully, waiting for her father to bring her breakfast. Her hands clench and unclench at the sides of the mattress. When she stops humming, the room is hush, like a memorial to her.

In the bathroom she showers for a long time, skimming the English Leather over the hills and valleys of her body. Her breasts hurt when she presses them. Her tan halts at her elbows and knees. She has the arms of a juvenile shot-putter, the calves of a bicycle rider. A week of missed lunches hasn't made any difference that she can see. But maybe today will: maybe, after today, many things will alter. When she's dried and dressed herself, Plum spends a short time with the objects, distilling their energy, whispering voodoo. Rearranging their positions inside the briefcase, something makes her think of Maureen. Maureen is like the objects come to life — she is happiness, she is power. The thought occurs that the objects brought Maureen to Plum: talismans, soaked through with feeling, must be capable of doing unguessable things. She closes the briefcase lid with more than her usual care.

Her mother drives her to Sophie's house at the arranged time. Plum is quiet on the journey, answering her mother's chatter with grunts. As she walks up the driveway of Sophie's home, she can feel her mother watching her. Although her heart is thudding, Plum is not tempted to run back to Mums and be comforted. At such times she knows herself to be a very determined girl. She knocks on the front door and, as it is opened, turns and waves a succinct good-bye.

Rachael, Dash and Samantha have already arrived; Plum suspects they conspired to arrive earlier, and her alienation entangles her like wire. But she reminds herself of why she's come, and shoves the disgruntlement down. This afternoon they are all here for her, in ways they cannot imagine. The longer they have been here, the more they've given her.

With the arrival of Caroline and Victoria, an urgency lights the edges of the afternoon. Sophie's parents won't be away forever, and her younger brother and sister will become nosy before long. Gripping her wrists, the friends propel Plum down the hall, crowding her into the bathroom. Sophie bellows, "Stay out!" to her siblings, and slams shut the door.

The bathroom into which Plum has been pushed is sunless and small, with a rectangular frosted window and a smell of rotten wood. The taps and rails are enameled white, the tiles are holiday-yellow. The decorations are aquatic—fish on the shower curtain, coral on the shelves. It makes Plum think of Cydar's bungalow, although the two rooms have really nothing in common. She fights down a fluttery desperation to be there, in the bungalow's bubbly gloom, hearing Cydar's wolf-voice explain. He's told her that a sea horse is difficult to keep alive in captivity; in Sophie's bathroom there's a dead one, a prickly husk hooked by the snout to the rim of the toothbrush holder.

The bathroom has already been organized for the operation. There's a high-backed chair in the center of the room, a hard bare arrangement of planks. Samantha slaps its seat, "Sit, sit." Plum sits, her heart galumphing like a pony in a sack. "Caz, Vics," says Samantha, "you'll need to hold her down. She'll probably try to run."

"I won't," Plum corrects. "You don't need to hold me."

"Well, if you struggle, you know what will happen. A needle in the eye."

Plum blasts the big blonde with hatred, then quickly retracts it. *Strength.* "I won't," she vows.

The confines of the bathroom mean that the friends

must crowd around the chair, and there's a warmth in the closeness of their bodies that vanishes the moment a gap opens between them, a yellow tile is seen; then the room becomes instantly frigid, and the girl on the chair shivers. Plum's hair is bundled into a shower cap, her shoulders are draped with a towel. "There won't be much blood." Sophie reassures her with a pat. "But just in case." Ice is brought and tipped into the basin, where it begins to melt. "I'm not touching her disgusting ears." Dash's lip can't curl higher. "I'm only here to watch. Don't ask me to do anything." So Sophie and Caroline each take charge of an ear, pressing ice cubes to the lobes. The coldness is a drilling pain that scrabbles at the nerves of Plum's teeth. She screws her eyes shut and endures what she can; then, "Wait!" she gasps, and digs the towel furiously into each earhole. "Are you numb?" asks Rachael.

"Numb in the head," says Dash. Plum squeezes a lobe consideringly. It feels peculiar, detached from her. "Just a bit more, maybe."

She sits with her hands clasped in her lap, ankles together and head high. The girls bob around her like bridesmaids. They are wearing their best casual clothes — knickerbockers, polo shirts, lolly-colored plastic sandals. Her friends have dressed up because of Plum, this afternoon exists because of her, the subject of their discussion is Plum — when they say *she,* they mean Plum. But Plum, silent and single-minded on the chair, is merely their object — she's a Christmas tree, a hunk of meat, merely the source of today's entertainment.

Plum feels the betrayal of her dignity, and it's nearly enough to make her cry. But *power,* she consoles herself: safety, place. She has a plan, and she concentrates on it.

Sophie pinches an earlobe. "Feel that?"

Plum does, but the sensation is muffled, and such deadness will do.

Victoria says, "I'll draw the dots."

A dot of marker is applied to each lobe, and criticized as uneven, then redecided as even. Plum, given a hand-mirror, stares at her image. Her broad forehead, her mane of hair, the round chin, the dark eyes. None of it seems familiar, it's the face of an emotionless enemy. The dots balance well enough, and Plum nods. "Show me again," says Sophie, and Plum looks up. "It's good," her friend tells her.

There is a candle burning in a holder, a burned-feather smell from the striking of the match. Now Samantha is holding a needle to the flame — a thick silver sewing needle, the kind over which Plum's fingers blunder in Needlework. The little fire dodges and ducks around the point. Plum squirms, plunging through nervousness and into real fear. Caroline glances at her, smiling tightly. "Don't worry," she says. Victoria says, "Hurry."

When Samantha douses the needle in water the steel should sizzle, but it does not. The bridesmaids fall back like the petals of a flower, and Plum is engulfed by yellow chill. "We could use two needles," Caroline suggests, a tinge of desperation in her voice. "Do both ears at once?"

"No," says Sophie. "It would hurt too much."

Samantha steps forward. "Lift your head." And although her body spasms with her treachery, although her heart kicks and whinnies, Plum raises her chin. She feels Samantha's manly fingers pincer the lobe; then, in a lull, nothing. The first thing that comes is sound, not pain. A burrowing, excavating sound. Then, "Ow!" Plum says. "Ow-ow-ow-ow—"

"Oh, yuck." Victoria hides her mouth.

"Wah wah wah wah!" A crow's noise warbles unstoppably from Plum. Knuckles dig into her cheek as Samantha leans closer—Plum hears her teeth grit, feels her fist push and turn. Fiery pain skims Plum's scalp, spears into her eyes and sinuses, bucks the wisdom teeth buried in her jaw. Her feet dance electrically on the linoleum. "Uk! Uk! Uk! Arh! Arh! Arh!"

"Hurry up, Sam!" Rachael shouts. "Put her out of her misery!"

Samantha's hand pivots; pain shoots through Plum's brain, accompanied by the sickening noise: "There!" says Samantha, stepping back. "That's one done. You've got fat ears, Aria."

Plum feels the needle prized backward, then the snub-nosed probing of the earring. Her lids, fiercely scrunched, are painful to unfurl. Through swirling vision she sees Victoria and Sophie staring; Caroline, behind her, pats her head. "There, there," she says.

Samantha crosses to Plum's other side, needle drawn

like an arrow. "Wait!" says Plum; she can't help but say it. "I don't—I can't—I don't want to!"

Her hands quaver, ready to fight. Samantha looks down at her, her face remorseless as a goddess's. "Only boys have one earring, Aria. Only boys . . . and girls who love girls." And though Plum isn't sure exactly what Samantha means, she does recognize the scorn that crouches, tail whipping, inside the words. "All right then," she moans.

Only later will the friends realize that they should have applied more ice at this point, for the left ear has considerably thawed; and by the time the needle is partway on its mission Plum has started to bawl, openmouthed like an infant, heedless of snot and drool. "Shut up!" Samantha bellows, but Plum cannot shut up: her body arches, her feet slither, tears rush from her eyes. And when it is over and Caroline says, "Your tongue was waggling like a lizard, Plummy," Plum has no strength remaining for shame. She slumps on the seat, hands clamped to her head, wondering if she might vomit. And yet, even as she hunches and gasps, the pain begins to withdraw, ebbing out of her skull to pool in her lobes—a fact Plum keeps to herself, for it's important that she appear ominously damaged. She squeezes her eyes so tears drop to her thighs, and shudders theatrically. "Are you OK?" Victoria asks her. Dash scoffs: "It couldn't have hurt that much. Your ear is just gristle, it's nothing. It would hardly have hurt at all."

But Plum's face, when she lifts it, is sufficiently stricken to make Dash close her know-it-all mouth. "Can I see the mirror?"

The mirror is hastily presented, and Plum studies. The two gold studs—perhaps more gray than gold—sit perkily in her lobes. There is no blood, but her ears are scarlet roses planted on each side of her head. She is now a girl with pierced ears. "Thanks, Sam," she whispers.

It is when she stands that her knees buckle, as had the knees of the lady at Justin's twenty-first birthday party; and exactly as Justin's friends had done, Plum's friends swoop to catch her. "I'll be OK." Plum lists groggily. "Maybe if I lie down . . ."

A delicious panic accompanies the girls as they scuttle their casualty down the hall to Sophie's bedroom. "She's just feeling faint," Rachael explains. "She's not dying, everyone!"

"Do you want water, Aria? Do you want ice cream?"

Plum, on the bed, waves a lank hand. "Just leave me alone for a minute. I just want to rest here a minute . . ."

And her friends abandon their victim with alacrity, swinging the door behind them. For a few minutes Plum lies like a weighty beast slain, her eyes roving Sophie's bedroom. It is a smaller room than Plum's, but the flooring is carpet rather than boards, and the cupboard is not a hefty thing like hers, but made-to-measure, with mirrored doors. She imagines her friends huddling elsewhere in the house, recounting the ordeal as if they too had spilled blood, not even allowing her to be the sole possessor of pain. Plum sniffs and sighs, wipes her nose and sits up. Immediately her gaze falls on what she has endured all this to find.

And when, some minutes later, Sophie knocks gently on the door, she finds Plum propped on her elbows, wan but full of forgiveness, and even pleased about what has been done.

That evening Plum sits on her own bed in her own bedroom, the briefcase open on her knees. A smile crosses her face irregularly, she prods the precious objects with the tips of her fingers. She's cozy with the smugness of success. Rachael, Samantha, that awful Dash: they think they are incredibly clever, but this afternoon at Sophie's they had not suspected what was going on. The real Plum had stood untouched, laughing at them. The actor Plum had been so good at almost fainting that she might do it again one day, perhaps when there's some compulsory school sports gala to attend.

Snug with satisfaction, she closes the case, shutting light from the icons. The latches catch with their safe sound, *chock chock.* Before going downstairs Plum checks to make sure her hair is covering her ears. Her lobes are throbbing, and feel thick as mice. If she squeezes them, fluid swells out from the pinpoint holes. In exchange for what she's achieved, the mutilation is fair. But she won't show it to anyone until the redness is gone, the leaking has stopped, and the difference looks like it didn't hurt at all.

She watches him walk toward the house, furtive but certain, easy to mistake for a thief. But she is not owned by anyone; what he gets, she gives gladly.

Except, of course, she had not meant to give love. It was meant to be amusement and now it is love, catastrophic as quicksand. She loves him, so much so that even the shirt he wears — a lime polo sporting the image of a cavorting snake-limbed bottle, with the words *Every Day is a Beer Barn Day!* printed across the shoulders — is not repulsive to her.

She can never quite believe the sight of him, his height, his smell, his groomed darkness, here in her hall — yet she feels she was born to see him. They meet at the door, where the carpet is protected by a loop-pile mat. Glancing down she notes that the skirting-board paint has been chipped. So this is not Paris or a steamy train station; nonetheless, it is wonderful. His presence makes it wonderful. She steps back, her hands enclosing his. She can't stop smiling in these first minutes, she's so buoyed and reassured. "We've got the afternoon to ourselves. Your sister is babysitting David. The *whole afternoon*," she marvels: it's like a year, like freedom. "Let's go out to lunch—"

"No," says Justin.

Maureen pauses—freezes, alert to the slightest change in pressure. "Is something wrong?"

"No." Then, because he knows what's been detected and because he wanted it to be, "I wish you wouldn't ask Plum to mind David."

She breathes again, her blood rushing on. "Your sister is perfectly capable—"

He won't let her misunderstand. "We shouldn't drag Plum into this."

Maureen steps back, raising stringent eyebrows—she knows the effect is like brandishing knives. If she had a knife she would aim it at him, not threateningly but enough to illustrate how close he's come to hurting her feelings. "This isn't mud. We're not *dragging* anyone into anything."

They are standing at the door of the master bedroom—when Maureen thinks of this room, she thinks of him. When he isn't here, she can still see him pulling back the bed's cover. She sees the puddle of his clothes, the opened belt and overturned shoes, his hand on the snowy sheet.

He rests his temple against the doorframe, and she will think of this too. From now on, when she passes the door, she'll think of him, and what he is about to say. If she had the knife she would press it warningly to the beer bottle dancing over his heart. He says, "You don't have to send David away."

Maureen laughs; and hates him a little. "David hasn't been *sent away*. He's having a day out with Aria. And we can go out too, like normal people."

"But we're not normal, are we? We have to hide all the time. We have to lie —"

"What lies? I don't lie. I never lie about you. I tell you openly that I love you."

He has long lashes that dip over his eyes because he can't look at her, at her coal-cool gaze or at her mouth which is a challenging red line. She stares an instant longer, then smiles, letting him off the hard hook. She had planned to take him to a restaurant, she's even bought a shirt for him to wear; but something has spooked him today, and it's clear they must stay with what's familiar. Maureen knows she tends to rush ahead, but only because the future looks so inviting. "Come," she says, scooping up his hands. Everything can be repaired. But as she steps into the bedroom, Maureen feels a resistance in his wrists — a moment of refusal which is there and gone so quickly that, were she to confront him with it, Justin could easily deny it, and she would have no choice but to believe.

* * *

Cydar is stunned by the sight of the boy. Maureen Wilks's son is sitting at the Coyle dinner table with a plate of soldier-cut sandwiches before him, tiny against the great pew and the vast tabletop, peaceful as a dust beam, and his presence can only mean that worlds have catastrophically collided—and all the while Cydar has been feeding sea monkeys to the angelfish, unaware of even a tremor. He pauses: "Hello. What are you doing here?"

But instead of demanding that Cydar confess what he knows, all Plum says is, "This is David, from next door. I'm babysitting."

"He's just turned four," announces Fa.

Cydar comes cautiously closer, into the shadows overhanging the table. Mums shuffles sideways, and he sits beside her. "I know David. Hi."

The boy considers him but says nothing, a snowflake hand feeding a sandwich into his mouth. Plum says, "We're going for a walk after lunch, aren't we? Then maybe we can see Cydar's fishes. Would you like that, Davy? To see the fish?"

"The clown fish?" Fa speaks loudly. "They're called clown fish, but they don't look like clowns. They don't have hats or red noses. And the eel? A big old eel like a long black sock."

The boy's gaze cruises his audience while he painstakingly chews up the sandwich. When the child's glance touches her, Cydar feels his mother twitch. He's always thought that Mums could have lived happily without her offspring—there are many things she's interested in besides them. She is what Cydar is, a distant heart, and her children and husband are things she chooses to tolerate, like rare parrots nesting in the chimney. When the boy looks at Mums, however, Cydar feels something strike in her—something too hot and too tender, a thing that makes his mother look away. *Wishing*, Cydar sees. And in his tightly stoned state he has a profound realization: Everyone in his family is sad. Mums and Fa, living lives that never managed to rise above the ordinary. Plum and Justin, aware of the peril, but neither of them clever enough to avoid a similar fate. Cydar himself, who will achieve enough for all of them, but will never feel rightly made for the world. Through the wide halls and spacious rooms of the house waft sorrows as vintage as antiques. "What do you want to eat at your party?" Mums is asking Plum, while, in the seat beside her, her son expires inside.

"Nothing homemade," Plum reiterates. "For snacks: Twisties, popcorn, chips. For lollies: Jaffas, Eclairs, Fantales, chocolate aniseed rings."

"Coke? Lemonade?"

"No, I want the punch you made at Christmas, the one with pineapple and ginger beer. But not too many bits of fruit in it. They get all soggy and disgusting."

"Not too much fruit," memorizes Mums.

Cydar's eyes seek out the child, who is contemplating the last honey soldier. A slim mop-haired boy *like a little old dog* is how Justin described him. *He'll leave home as soon as he can pack a bag.* Cydar starfishes a hand on the table, the oak under his palm as slick as kelp; David considers with interest the onyx stone worn on the starfish's ring finger, the curl of silver in the image of a snake coiling around the finger alongside it. Cydar flexes his hand so the snake strikes—the boy obligingly smiles. Justin will surely see this child sitting in the kitchen for exactly what he is: a black sign. A crack that will tear open to inundate everything, not *if,* but when. "Don't eat that sandwich if you're not hungry, David," Cydar tells him.

"No, he's probably had enough." Fa is shouting now. His pleasure in the boy's presence is painful. It occurs to Cydar that when the truth rushes through their house, this is where his parents' sympathies will fly: to the son who is not their own. The one whose potential is not yet threadbare, who can yet perhaps offer hope. "We can give your sandwich to the birdies in the park," Plum tells the child; and there follows one of the oddest moments that Cydar has ever known, when for an instant the whole room seems to quake with a yearning that pours out from the people inside it, a lack that desperately wants comforting but meets only empty air. While the moment holds, no one moves or says anything, and Cydar fears he might stumble from the kitchen like Munch's screamer, fingers gouged into his cheeks.

"What else?" Mums asks then. "A barbecue?"

Plum looks at her. "What else? Hot dogs!" And everyone is again their enduring selves. "Hot dogs, garlic bread, vol-au-vents with chicken. Ice-cream cake—chocolate, I hate strawberry. For breakfast the next morning, pancakes. Do you know how to make pancakes? If you're not sure, you should practice. I don't want hopeless pancakes at my party . . ." Plum pauses, pulling at her hair. Her gaze skates around the table before fixing on her brother. "Don't forget you said you'd come to the party, Cydar."

"Did I?"

"You know you did." Her voice is iron. "You promised."

Knowing all, he understands this isn't just her usual bossiness. Something hulks behind her insistence, and it's darkly important to her. Some adolescent melodrama is occurring in his sister's world; the Wilks boy's presence in the Coyle kitchen testifies to what Justin has allowed *his* world to become. Only Cydar, it seems, lives a quiet life, a garden snail's honest existence. "It's all right," he says. "I'll be there."

The ceiling of the bedroom is elaborately mapped with a plasterwork pattern that reaches out geometrically into the corners of the room. Justin studies the interlocking rectangles while Maureen talks. She, too, is facing the ceiling, but only Justin sees it. He knows Maureen dislikes the decoration—it doesn't suit what she's trying to do with the house. She needs smooth ceilings, canvas light-shades. The ceiling survives the way it is only because her husband likes it. The fact, recollected, makes Justin look away, like an altar boy encountering a sleeping priest. He hardly knows Bernie Wilks and doesn't think of his neighbor often; but when he does, Justin does not see him as an enemy or even a rival, but rather as a confederate. A picture sometimes comes to Justin, of himself and Bernie Wilks talking through the dense stone of a cell wall. It is *Papillon,* it is *Cool Hand Luke,* it's *The Great Escape.* It is strange.

Maureen has said something. When Justin turns his head to her, the pillow sighs a vanilla scent. "Barcelona or Rome or Berlin?"

It's easier to simply choose than to query what he's choosing. He selects what seems the most unlikely, the least trampled road. "Berlin."

She rolls over to face him, her mouth very close. "Let's catch a plane to Berlin. We'll rent an empty warehouse near the zoo. It will have big dirty windows and a timber floor, and high ceilings like a cathedral. We'll have no furniture except a bed, and we'll wear nothing but black — black suits, black hats, black boots. We'll only be friends with artists. In winter we'll hibernate in the only room we can afford to heat, eating sauerkraut. We'll have a little stove for boiling water, and we'll grind our own coffee beans."

Justin looks up at the plasterwork metropolis, carried as if her words were wings to a dusty loft in an elusive city, a wide window overlooking an avenue of elms. He sees himself standing behind the glass, a mug of coffee in one hand, a hand-rolled cigarette in the other. He seems, in this vision, to be wearing a beret.

"I'll run a gallery. It's what I've always wanted to do. The artists will bring me their paintings, and I'll sell them to people who deserve them."

She nuzzles his shoulder, her weight against his ribs. He asks, "What will I do?"

"You can buy a guitar and busk at railway stations." He sees the beret openmouthed on the ground. "And in the evenings you can model nude for the artists."

The idea makes her laugh merrily, kicking her long legs so the sheet billows off their bodies, puffing out a sweaty scent. Justin catches her hand, holds it against his chest. The ceiling above him is all whiteness and angles, like snow on the roofs of a Bavarian village. He knows nothing about Bavaria, Berlin, artists or guitars, he can think of no more dire prospect than spending his life in a warehouse with Maureen, but he can chuckle and unfold a daring map of life because it is only words, nothing will happen, he is quite safe. Yet it's something that has always charmed him about Maureen, her belief that he is capable of doing and being anything. To her, he has more promise than he'd ever have use for. To her, he's not just a man like any other. He might miss this feeling when it's gone. "You'd get tired of me," he says. "You'd get bored, and run off with some foreigner."

"I would never be bored. Maybe by sauerkraut. Not by you." She presses nearer so her breast lies against him, her breathing shifts his hair. "You can fall asleep, Justin. I would like to watch you sleeping."

But sleep would signal the acceptance of something. "No, I should go."

"Stay one more minute." She begs it as usual. And although he should shake her off, make a stand, he does not; he lies as if paralyzed, his gaze seeking out the Escheresque pattern above his head. "We could hitchhike to the Black Forest." She speaks tickingly against his chest. "Eat cake."

"Hmm." He has no lingering interest.

"They bombed the Berlin zoo during the war, you know. Blew the elephants to pieces."

"Well," he says, "we won't go then." Ten more minutes, and he's home.

Plum holds David's hand as they walk, feeling the faith within the curled paw. Inside her there's blooming a sense of pride that she has been judged capable by him. Guarding the child, she's like a girl who's arrived to save the world.

It is autumn, but it still feels like summer. The sun is like an angry dog, and they move quickly from shade to shade. Plum does not want him to be bored so she unspools a running commentary about birds, clouds, colors, pets, trees, shoes. David is not a talkative boy but he listens, his face turned up like a flower; and when she asks him a question he replies matter-of-factly after giving brief thought to the answer. He trips along the footpath beside her, his small arm forming a right-angle up to her hand, and Plum realizes with some shock that she feels different in his company. It's not like being with her friends at school. It's not like sitting at the dinner table. With him, she is just she. It's a weightless feeling, like dragging off muddy gumboots and leaving them at the door.

They go to the playground, having skirted the oval carefully, discussing the danger of bees. As usual the playground is deserted, so they have the equipment to themselves. Tanbark crumples underfoot, huffing out tawny dust. "The slide?" David asks, and Plum says, "No, it's too hot." To illustrate she puts her palms on the metal, which is scorching as a skillet, and dances about yelping. David mulls over this, suggests, "Maybe the swing?"

So she lifts him onto the swing and pushes him back and forth while the child grips the chains and says nothing, stoically enjoying the ride. Plum finds a rhythm, and her thoughts wander. She remembers the day before, lying alone in Sophie's bedroom, knowing her friends were in the kitchen discussing her, someone about whom they know nothing. She'd felt so clever in those few minutes—ruthless *happiness,* pitiless *power*—but now, swinging the child, it all seems pathetic. Why does she care so much? What does it matter if her friends don't like her? After all, she hates them. Tomorrow she'll stop hanging around with them. She will step out of their coven and purify into a lone dove. Become the kind of girl who doesn't care what other girls think. The kind who sits in the quadrangle at lunchtime reading a book. The one whose surname you can't remember when writing names on the flipside of the school photograph. The one beside whom only a teacher will sit on the bus, en route to an excursion.

And Plum is frightened, and shunts the idea from her mind.

She lets the swing simmer until the child is able to step off. There's a cage of crisscrossing metal bars over which he runs to swarm. Plum, fanning her face, flops on the bench in the shade. She is muggy in the underarms, there's a napkin of sweat between the nubbins, another dampening her shoulder blades. Her hands and face feel swollen, even her eyes seem to bulge: she is such a beast. She has been throwing away her lunch for a week, enduring daily the ravages of starvation, yet still she is a monster. She shuts her eyes, which is mercy of a sort. Her hands creep up to rest on her ears. In the mirror this morning the lobes had been red, exuding heat like hot-water bottles—except, when she had touched them the lobes weren't pliable, as hot-water bottles are. They were firm as muscle. When she'd flicked them, they hadn't wobbled, and they don't wobble now. Touching them spills a blunt-nosed pain into her skull. She rotates the studs as instructed, and meets a sticky resistance that can't be right. "Poo," she mutters. "Oh, poo . . ."

"Poo," the word echoes: Plum's eyes startle open. David is standing beside her, clutching a piece of tanbark. Plum doesn't know how big a child should be, but David seems tiny, a doll. He has a doll's glossy hair, pink lips and exaggerated eyes. His head is tipped sideways with inquisitiveness. "I've got sore ears," she tells him. "My friends pierced my ears, and it hurt and hurt, and now my ears are sore and I might get sick . . . "

Tears, which so frequently swell behind her joys and her furies, squirm out and run down her cheeks. She's ugly, she's fat, her friends hate her—she hates herself. The first tear plunges through the wooden slats of the bench. "I wish I was four, like you," she moans. "Look at my ear, Davy—look!"

She pushes back her hair, and the lobe is a mirror turned to the sun, a source of bushfires and global catastrophe. David, however, does not flinch. From the corner of an eye Plum watches him study the wounded appendage thoughtfully. Then, like a sniffing animal, he edges closer, so close she feels the air feathering from him. When his lips brush the convex shell of her ear, a tingle runs down her spine. He steps back in silence, gripping the tanbark with both hands, and Plum stares at him in wonder. "Thank you," she says. "I think my ears will get better now."

The sky is too blue, it is too hot to stay. She climbs off the bench and takes his hand. They do not cross the oval, but opt for the side street that will loop them home. Aside from the bees, there's no reason to take this longer route; with the sun above and the child beside her, there are good reasons not to. But when she sees Justin's car, Plum knows why she chose that path. She wants to see the car exist in another's eyes.

The Holden is parked in the same place as before, underneath the paperbark opposite the house with the gnome. Its tires aren't flat, it is stopped neatly against the gutter, the chrome around its headlights flares with recent polishing. The two children stand before the vehicular mystery, Plum swinging David's arm. "What's Justin's car doing here?" she asks the trees, the oxygen, the life-force, the child.

"I don't know," says David.

"Don't you?" Plum sighs. "I don't either."

ᴔ ON MONDAY MORNING her friends flock to her; it's not her they want to see, but their handiwork. "Ugh." Victoria sticks out her tongue. "It looks infected."

"It's not infected!" Samantha squawks. "Everything was clean, you saw it!"

Plum stands like a cow in a yard while her friends mill about her. Their Monday-morning uniforms smell clean and freshly ironed. They are gathered in the thoroughfare of the locker corridor, and around them parts a noisy tide of girls burdened by bags as unwieldy as rhinos, armed with spiked plates of textbook. Plum is bumped and knocked, scuffed and buffeted. Caroline's face puckers at Plum's cauliflowered head. "Does it hurt?"

Plum nods briefly, as one for whom suffering is inevitable.

Sophie says, "My ears didn't look like that after I got them pierced. Mine didn't go all purple."

"Well aren't you so *special*." The assembly bell is ringing, and Samantha wheels away. "There's nothing wrong, Aria!" she yells over a shoulder. "In a few days you'll be fine! Stop sooking!"

"I wasn't sooking," Plum points out — but her friends are dispersing, flicking away like minnows into the crowd, and a strong broad girl whom Plum doesn't know advises her curtly, "Out of the way, idiot."

On the bus ride home there's a moment in which the bubble that is Plum's self-confidence seems unable to rise, and the prospect is that, even at home, she will feel weak and unwanted. This has never happened before. Arriving home, she heads straight to her room, where she retrieves the briefcase with urgency. She touches each object, balances their weights, compresses them inside her hands. Today the coin is her least favorite. She has tried to befriend the coin, admire it, see good in it, but has failed. The coin is ugly, and should never have been minted. She wonders if a coin can be burned or melted. She conjures a force field around her body, tells the coin in a monotone, "I cause you pain I cause you pain."

She rocks on her haunches, craving to run to Maureen — Maureen who is always pleased to see her, who is a river, rather than a war — but the Datsun Skyline is parked in the driveway like a great blue tumor. That man is a pest. Instead she lies on her bed flipping through an encyclopedia of movies, thinking about her birthday, her upcoming party, the many potholes in her life. Her bag-of-concrete body. Her ball-of-fire ears.

On Tuesday at lunchtime, Sophie is crying. It is not Plum's shoulder upon which her old friend chooses to weep, so Plum does as Rachael and Caroline are doing, and hovers in the background being concerned. "What is it?" they ask Victoria, when Sophie has recovered enough to stumble off to the tuckshop for a Wagon Wheel. Victoria explains that Sophie has lost the bracelet of which she's been so proud, and Caroline gasps, "Oh no! Lost already? Father Christmas only just gave it to her!"

Plum stares after Sophie, keeping her thoughts to herself. Her friend has lost a treasure, but she still gets to go to the tuckshop. She doesn't have to throw her lunch in the bin. Sophie goes home to her carpeted bedroom with its mirrored cupboard doors, and she doesn't spend the night worrying if her friends will still be her friends in the morning. She can buy another treasure, and it will be the same as if she'd never lost the original. Things could be worse, but Sophie's the type who'll never know.

The girls don't ask to see Plum's ears, and she doesn't offer to show them. Today it feels as if rabbits have buried their teeth in her lobes. At home, unbelievably, the Datsun is in the driveway. "Go away!" Plum seethes. "Can't you see nobody wants you?" She slams downstairs to take out her frustrations on her mother, pawing roughly through the frozen food that Mums has bought for the party. Blissfully, a scandal: "I told you *chicken* vol-au-vents! No one in the world likes *tuna*!" It is so upsetting that she flings herself upstairs again, thumping the wall as she goes. She squeezes her ears — she is drawn to molesting them — and the pain makes her clutch at her skull.

At lunchtime on Wednesday, Plum is lunar. She sits with her friends underneath the oak, floating above their debate about the strictness of Victoria's dad, her mind as shifty as the northern lights she's heard about in Geography. She's hungry — she's a helium balloon — and thinks about unearthing her sandwich from the bin. Her ears are raw protuberances as angry as the creature in *Eraserhead*. She is staring vacantly across the quadrangle, a clump of straw in the shape of a sad girl, when something happens, and partially revives her. Rachael, Samantha and Dash have a hump-backed powwow about the present they're clubbing together to buy her. Rachael glances up from the huddle, warns, "Don't listen, Aria!" And Plum, returned to earth, is surprised to find that the mood is good, that she's welcome among them today. "Where's your lunch, Plummy?" Caroline asks. "Did you forget to bring it?" And although Plum is picky, and prefers not to eat food prepared by fingers that might not be clean using knives that mightn't have been properly washed, she accepts half of Caroline's salami sandwich, and it makes her want to cry.

That afternoon she sits against her bedhead, the briefcase

on her knees. The wristwatch with its fine band is like a bird's skeleton. The fastening pin of the Abba badge is still spiky and well-sprung. Today the yo-yo is her favorite, but she feels kind toward them all.

Maureen walks in the garden after dinner, and it's a miracle: Plum pulls on her sandals and runs. "Hello, hello!" she warbles, rushing up her neighbor's drive. The garden is a glade still dripping from the hose — Maureen stands out against the lawn like an orchid, all lankiness and waxen beauty. "David's asleep?" Plum is disappointed. Over the past few days she's found her mind returning to their afternoon at the playground. "Thank goodness," says Maureen. "He's been under my feet all day. Would you take him again this Saturday? For a few hours in the evening?"

"OK," says Plum.

"You'll be rich! You can buy new clothes. . . ."

"I wanted to get my ears pierced," Plum reminds her. "But I don't need to do that anymore."

Her earlobes have become a treacherous reef of concern, something around which Plum has been trying to maneuver as if they are merely an inconvenience, secretly fearing they're about to rip the hull from her. Her ears aren't getting better, and the logical consequence of leaving them to fester is first tragic and then terrifying. Instead of a birthday party, the casualty ward. In common with Mr. Potato Head, a pair of plastic ears. She needs relief from the secrecy, aid for the agony: she needs Maureen. Sheepishly she draws her hair aside to expose her ears. Maureen's mouth makes a circle of appreciation on seeing the bossy studs. Then she looks closer. "They're infected, Aria."

"I know . . ."

"Did you do this yourself?"

"My friends did."

"With what? A rusty nail?" Maureen recoils. "Those wretched girls! You silly child! Why would you let them maim you? You're not their *plaything,* Aria! Have you shown your mother? Have you been to a doctor?" She prods a lobe with a fingernail. "Oh, Aria!"

"I haven't shown anyone," the girl says meekly; and even in her outrage, Maureen hears what this means. *You are vital.* "Please don't tell Mums."

The distaste seeps from the woman's face; she draws the girl to her, inspects the damage carefully. Plum keeps her gaze down while Maureen's arms move around her, her breasts shuffling close to her face. Her friend's fingers feel cool against the fire-filled lobes. Methylated spirit is fetched from the house, along with a clutch of tissues: these are applied, dripping and stinging, until the earrings can be eased from their niches. "Cheap things," scorns Maureen, tossing them into the garden. "Never wear cheap jewelry, Aria, it lessens your worth." She dabs with the tissues, smoothing aside Plum's hair, and the smell of the spirit is a physical entity, hot and cold at the same time. It smarts, but Plum can feel the infection contracting like a tick from a flame. She keeps her eyes closed and savors the garden around her, the soft evening air, the tranquilizing touch of the woman's hands.

Suddenly it is finished: "Take the methylated spirit home with you," says Maureen, "and use it whenever you can."

Plum opens her eyes reluctantly. "What about earrings?" The hard-won holes will close without them.

"One thing at a time," Maureen replies.

"Will I be all right?" She can't shake the image of plastic ears.

"Yes, you will. If not, I'll take you to a doctor. Your mother doesn't need to know."

Plum sways slightly. "Thank you."

Maureen crosses the lawn to the tap. "And besides receiving a dose of tetanus from your friends," she says, "how have you been? How is everything at home?"

Now that she is no longer the sole caretaker of her ears, everything seems revitalized to Plum. "Good! Mums has bought the party food. I'm still not eating my lunch. I'll be getting skinnier soon." Then, scouting, she remembers something interesting — the Holden parked in the obscure street. "That Justin's up to something, I think."

"What do you mean?" Maureen shuts off the tap.

Plum hesitates, trying to see beyond the car, to hear what the car is saying; but she's deafened by the scantness of her experience, blind to the horizons of a young man. She attempts, instead, to be cryptic. "He's got a secret he's not telling. I'm not sure if it's a good thing or a bad thing: but I think it might be a bad thing."

"A bad thing! You're very dramatic. Maybe it's — a girlfriend?"

"No, I don't think so." Plum shakes her head slowly. "He always shows off when he's got a girlfriend. He talks about her all the time, takes *her* to the movies instead of me, invites her over for dinner. If he had a girlfriend, he wouldn't keep it secret. He wouldn't tell lies about a girlfriend."

"How do you know he's telling lies?"

"Because he says he's going to work, but he isn't."

It sounds, she hopes, like the flipping of an ace card. Maureen stands on the lawn, her skirt wavering, wiping her hands together. "So what do you think is happening?" she asks.

"I don't know. I'm not sure." Plum, now she thinks on it, is really quite uneasy. She can't hear what the Holden is telling her, but something about it is foreboding. And she desperately doesn't want anything to be wrong for Justin — *she* can lie awake at night, skin crawling with dreadfulnesses, but it's unbearable to think of Justin doing the same. Plum would scatter her brother's life all over the lawn if it would make things good for him, if she actually had something to reveal; instead she must confine herself, lamely but at least mysteriously, to, "Whatever it is, it's bad."

Cydar's bungalow is one of Plum's favorite places, but she only visits rarely, aware of the consequences of making a nuisance of herself. He is home the following evening, looks up guardedly from his lecture notes when she knocks. He's a pale wraith in a corner, lit at the fringes by the beam of a desk lamp. "What?" he says. She asks, "Can I come in?" And because he doesn't say she can't, he means she may.

Cydar, like Mums, is a collector. The floor of the bungalow is padded with overlapping rugs, its walls are puzzled with pictures, and books stack like bricks along the skirting-board. Every found object, every gift, every coveted possession or passing whimsy is kept, each item imprisoned in its allotted place. Even the cigarette butts are pressed neatly into the ashtray, no flake of ash permitted to spill. Viewed from the doorway, it's a complicated, intriguing room, yet nevertheless only a room. But then the sound of the sea calls, compelling the visitor to turn.

From floor to ceiling, one wall of the bungalow is glass. The glass is divided into the rectangles of fish tanks that stand on a grid of steel shelves. The tanks are lit by white fluorescence that gleams off the gravel and emanates a foggy glow. The sea-sound comes from the relentless filtering of water through canisters packed with wool and charcoal; thrumming pumps force a trillion bubbles through the water, so the aquariums are as vibrant as bloodstreams. The bungalow should smell of cigarette smoke but instead the odor is of chemicals and aquarium water, a fluidy, vegetable smell. Most of the tanks are heated, which makes the bungalow dank and close. The lulling sound, the organic fragrance and the moist atmosphere combine into something like the laboratory in *The Island of Dr. Moreau,* an electrically powered womb.

And within the living whiteness are the beasts it keeps

alive. Catfish, angelfish, loaches of many kinds. Firemouths, tetras, gourami, idols, barbs; red-tailed sharks, a loaf-sized nurse shark, several candy-striped coral shrimp. Thirty or forty different types of creature—Plum can never keep track of them all. The fish patrol ceaselessly over rocks and coral, nibbling at vegetation. Every drifting particle catches their eye, is swallowed and spat out in a disgruntled purge. Occasionally there's action, a fish jolted by hair-trigger energy; then a chase might erupt, fish darting and slashing—before harmony returns just as suddenly, bestowing immediate calm.

Plum stands close to the glass, as visitors always do. Her gaze chips from fish to fish, as the gaze of an unpracticed watcher always does. She wonders what these animals mean to Cydar. They are pretty—striped and dashed and psychedelically smudged, their tails like chiffon—but pretty is all they seem to her. To him, they must be something more. She imagines her brother lying on his bed at night, the bungalow illuminated by the aquariums' haze, listening to the water churn and churn. He would watch the fish weaving between the weeds, investigating the rocks, rifling the gravel. Plum hears what Cydar would hear, sees what Cydar would see, but she can't understand what he thinks. Justin's car has been silent as a sphinx to her, and Cydar's fish slip through her fingers. It occurs to her that she lives in a house with people she knows only from the outside. That everything she thinks she knows about them has been a guess.

"What do you want?" Cydar asks.

The fish swim through Plum's reflected body, exactly as if she were drowned. "What's that?" She points to a luminous whip-beast she hasn't seen before.

"A neon goby."

"Good."

Cydar says, "Hmm."

"Where's my favorite?" She scans the wall for the bad-tempered destroyer, the night-blue jewel fish. There he is, close to the ceiling, swimming alone in the tank he has rendered a wasteland. A fighter not a lover, he can't have friends. Plum likes everything about him.

"I have a new favorite." Cydar gets up and comes to the tanks, his reflection clarifying alongside hers, a black snake beside a goose. He points out a fish, gray on the belly, darker on top. Its eyes are large, its tail trim, its whiskers half as long as itself. It sweeps the gravel without pause. "A shovel-nosed catfish."

Plum knows catfish are lowly, and there are more spectacular specimens on all sides. "What's so good about it?"

"Well, think. It's timeless. Shovel-nosed catfish looked just the same as that when they were picking the bones of drowned dinosaurs, Plum. When we were still rat-men hiding in trees."

"Aria."

He looks askance, as if he's never seen her before. "What?"

"It's Aria, not Plum. I told you."

With that, his enthusiasm evaporates; he returns to the desk, shakes a cigarette from its box, lights it with a sharply struck match. "What do you want?"

A yellow tang poises like a coin over Plum's reflected eye. She had come wanting only a few minutes of her brother's company, but suddenly she wants more. It has always been Justin and Cydar; she wants it to be Justin and Cydar and Plum. "Remember how I saw Justin's car parked near the playground the other day?"

"What about it?"

"I saw it there again on Sunday, when I took David to the swings."

Cydar draws on the cigarette, contemplating the tang, which is like an emperor's tea-saucer, a disc of flawless gold. "So?"

"*So?*" Plum spins to him. "It's funny, don't you think? Both days Justin said he was going to work — he got *dressed* for work, he said he'd be home for dinner *after work* — but both days his car wasn't anywhere *near* where he works."

The tang sails on without effort, an orange wrasse moving aside without argument to let it pass. The cigarette unspools smoke into the humid air, and when Cydar taps it on the ashtray, gray flakes break to reveal the burning hub. "It's funny," he agrees, "but probably none of your business."

"Cydar! It *is* my business if something's wrong —"

"No, it isn't. Justin's not a baby."

"Yes, but he's my brother — *your* brother too!"

A moment goes by before Cydar answers. He props on his desk smoking his cigarette, following the fish. Finally he says, "Whatever it is, my advice is leave it alone. You might make things worse. Then you'll wish you *had* stayed out of it. Won't you?"

Plum draws breath to deny this; then turns, frustrated, back to the fish. The fish, whose gravest concern is what their next meal will be — a concern to which Plum also used to give priority. Without even trying, she's collected more important things to bother about. "Justin's a grown-up," her brother consoles her. "You shouldn't worry about him."

"Hmph." Plum touches a finger to the warm glass. "But things go wrong for grown-ups, you know. They show bad things on TV all the time. And even if Justin was *really* old, I wouldn't want something horrible happening to him."

In the shadows, the tip of the cigarette glows as tropically as a fish. "It's only a car in a street, Aria. It's nothing."

"It's not nothing. It's something. And I know what it is."

Cydar lifts blackbird eyes. "What?"

"Justin's been fired." The explanation had come to her that morning, during Home Economics, the single solution that makes sense. She'd been creaming butter, and her hand had grown still. "He's lost his job at the bottle shop, and he's too ashamed to tell. So he gets dressed in his work shirt and drives away, and hides the car and goes off somewhere until it's time to come home."

Cydar smokes silently, his gaze traveling the tanks. The many legs of a coral shrimp flail like cut kite strings. Then he gives a short laugh and says, "That sounds like something Fa would do."

Plum's heart clutches, her hands go to her face. "Cydar! It's awful! What will we do?"

"I told you. Mind your business. Let Justin live how Justin likes."

"But" — she's stymied — "we should do *something* —"

Cydar smiles vexingly. "No. Learn a lesson from these fish, Aria: don't interfere. Whatever's happening, it's Justin's stuff. You're a kid: worry about kid stuff."

Plum scowls and looks away, glowering into the tanks. The aquariums are beautiful, like living pirate chests, almost too beautiful to be true. But what Cydar has learned after years of living amid such glory is something that seems ugly — that it's easier not to get involved. If she dared, Plum might disagree: but she doesn't, because Cydar is so clever that it's possible he is right. And although she's not a kid — not in the disparaging way her brother means; she's a real person, with feelings, and it's right for her to fret over Justin, who is the best thing in her world — she must stay on Cydar's good side. She's promised her friends he will be at the party. "You can call me Plum," she says; she's actually relieved now that she's accepted his advice, she feels like a pigeon who's flown a long distance and is finally home. "It's no good when you say Aria."

IT RAINS: THIS SEEMS APPROPRIATE. Justin dresses with characteristic attention to his clothes. He stands in front of the bathroom mirror, twitching his hair until it sits correctly, searching his jaw for missed whiskers. He adjusts his belt, straightens his creases, plucks a thread from a buttonhole. Whenever he can, he likes to look his best. Tonight, he thinks of this care as his gift.

Plum is watching television with David in the den. Justin steps down the staircase lightly, avoiding the loudest treads. "I think you *want* to get caught," Cydar had accused, having informed him that their sister had seen the Holden parked, yet again, in the same street. "That way, you can blame someone else for whatever happens." The unfairness of this had peeved Justin greatly. He *dreads* the prospect of discovery — all those questions that will demand to be answered, all those wounded looks and uncomfortable encounters to be endured — and now he creeps to the front door on tiptoe. He doesn't want David to see him. The child will chirp with recognition. Nor does he want to cross Plum's path — she will remind him that *Rosemary's Baby* is the late-late movie, and badger to know when he'll be home. The bolt makes a sound like knuckles when he turns it, and everything in Justin winces. And the wincing itself is appalling, a sign.

Outside, the rain coming down is cooling relief, although it ruins his hair.

Maureen has prepared a dinner complete with candles and aperitifs. It is their first proper meal together, he could not have refused; and he sees all the indications of its importance, the nice plates, the flowers, the artillery of forks and knives. He sees the hours in front of him. "Devils on horseback," she says, offering a plate to his chest. The concoction of prunes and bacon is the sort of thing Justin never eats — he has a shepherd's taste in food. She knows, but serves this anyway. Like a voice mumbling into a sleeping ear, she works to alter him. She thinks that alteration is what he wants, and what is good for him. And, at first, Justin had been eager to change. He'd wanted to be the kind of man this smarter, older woman might think equal. Now, though — now that Maureen's intelligence has so often proved a tedious test or trap, now the years that separate them have lost their power to intrigue, now he's witnessed her at her most basic, and it's lowered his awe to earth—it is humiliating to recall that old willingness. How easily impressed he had been. "Did you see David?" Maureen's asking, and he sips champagne from an anorexic glass and admits, "No. I hid."

"Hid? What for?"

"I didn't hide," he says, because it's simpler to inexplicably change the story, he can't be *bothered* following the path down which the admission will lead; and she doesn't remark on his apparent schizophrenia, she doesn't even seem to have heard. She is wearing a white jumpsuit which has a line of stainless-steel studs from breastbone to waist—he imagines the banging, like firecrackers, that would accompany the removal of the jumpsuit. Her feet are bare, which he would have once found enticing; now their calculated nakedness seems pitiful, worse than the exposing of an undesired breast. She glides close to him, and were it not for the devil in one hand and the glass in the other, she would try to make him waltz. She once suggested accompanying him to a club or a disco, somewhere they might dance. It has never happened, and it never will. "Look at you," she's saying. "Standing here, like you belong."

"Maybe I'm here too often."

"Hardly. What does your mother say? *Poo?*"

Justin smiles stickily. Cydar had said, "Something's not right about her." And it isn't right that she knows his mother's word, which belongs to Justin's childhood and to Justin's family. She hangs against his shoulder, a habit he no longer finds endearing; her open-necked collar channels his sights down her cleavage, and even this fails to please. He'll always think her body is beautiful; but he won't want it, in particular, anymore. "We've got your sister to thank for tonight," she's saying, and every word sounds like the ingredient of a potion. He struggles to slow this slide into aversion — he doesn't want to hate her, having once believed he loved her — but what's left of his affection tumbles downhill unstoppably. It has to end, it's already ended. He didn't know it when he knocked on the door, but he has come to say good-bye. "I don't know how we coped without Aria. She's a bonanza."

He's still smiling. "Maybe you shouldn't get too friendly with her."

"Justin! Aria's an innocent. She's completely without guile. It's just a bit of fun."

Justin swallows the champagne. *If she has Plum,* Cydar had warned, *she has a weapon.* And it had not sounded crazy. "What can she do?" Justin had asked. "She can't do anything. She'd risk losing too much." And Cydar, standing at the chest of drawers spinning the oddment bowl, replied, "*Rubber bands.* She might be willing to lose."

So it must be done, this very night — Justin's anxious, now, to have it done. Maureen is an anchor he hadn't meant to drop. There are rowdy companions, there are preferable girls, there are concerts and beaches, bars and sunrises, parties, hangovers, card tables, football games. There are scuffles in the street, cars to drive fast, half-remembered taxi rides into the beds of strangers. There are ways to live that don't involve lying, explaining, apologizing. The most energizing aspects of infatuation die suddenly, and make for embarrassing, inconvenient corpses. Between himself and Maureen the thrill is gone, what sparkled is stale, the need has extinguished. If things are different for Maureen, that is regrettable. He doesn't want to hurt her, he wants her to be happy, he's even prepared to stay friends, if that's what she wants. In fact, living side-by-side as they do, it will be easier if they're friends. But he doesn't need or love her, and any feelings Maureen has for him are her own responsibility: he won't be blamed for them. When he leaves, he won't be carrying anything with him.

"Maureen—" he begins.

The oven alarm yells raucously: Maureen grips his wrist and guides him to the dining table. "I hope you're hungry. It's apricot chicken." The table is a circular arrangement of chrome and smoked glass—it's hard to imagine eating a satisfying meal off such a thing. Justin sits alone, annoyed. The moment is lost, but he is resolved, he won't put it off another day. Maureen returns from the kitchen with plates on which repose flanks of chicken doused with sizzling apricot sauce. She brings brown rice in a clay tureen that has a decorative matching ladle. Justin pours while Maureen serves; when she sits, she raises her glass to him, and he hurriedly hoists his own. "You look handsome," she says. "Is that shirt new?" Such must be their conversation—they have no mutual friends, no shared occupations, no rich entwined history to review. He won't talk of the future, which belongs to him; of the present, so little remains to say. Forever after, Justin will credit Maureen with teaching him the startling fact that fucking alone doesn't make for sustainable conversation.

"Is the rice all right?"

"Yes, it's perfect."

"Not undercooked?"

"No, fine."

He feels her gaze moving over him. "I wish I could sit at this table with you every night."

Soon she'll be talking about divorce. Cydar had said it in the voice of a necromancer. They'd been sitting in the bungalow, stoned as pagans; Justin had laughed aloud. Marriage, infants, divorce, old age — these things don't concern him. Now, as he seeks the bone with the point of his knife, Justin feels a stab of unshirkable urgency. "Maureen," he says, "I think we should stop — this. I want to."

From across the iceland of table she stares at him, a cheetah reflected in glass. The first time he'd seen her, Justin had been stunned. He'd been mowing the naturestrip and she had strolled by with an envelope in her hand. Beneath the roar of the mower she'd spoken to him; he had shut off the motor, and she'd spoken again. New to the neighborhood, she couldn't find a postbox. He had given her directions, and they'd looked at each other. "Thank you," Maureen had said. A feather had flown up Justin's spine.

"No," she says. "Why should we?"

He can't say, *I'm cold.* "Think about it, Maureen. I like you—you know that. But it can't work—you know it can't."

"No, I don't know that." The cutlery in her hands is subsiding. "Are you saying it can't work because I'm married? Are you feeling guilty?"

He's felt lustful and swinish and craven and captured, overwhelmed and expanded and spirited and bored, but he's never felt guilty, not about anything. "Of course."

She answers immediately, "I'll leave him."

"No." It's all Justin can do not to scramble from his chair. "You can't do that. You've got this life. You've got this house. With me, you'd have nothing—"

"I'd have *you*. That's all I want." She sits back and she doesn't seem angry, just bemused by his failure to see what's plain. "It's not asking much, is it? One person, out of all the world?"

"But what about David?" The recollection of the child is a sudden spark in Justin's mind. "He needs you."

From across the table Maureen stares at him. Her knife and fork, slumping in her grip, have dotted the glass with apricot sauce. Outside, a car toots, shooing a cat off the road; from the record player in the corner comes a jazzy beat that Justin can't bear. "I don't understand." Her voice is flat now. "What's changed, Justin? Nothing. So why should *we* change? There's no need. No one knows. No one is being hurt—"

Justin snatches at this means of release. "But they *are*. People *are* being hurt."

"Hurt how?"

"Hurt because . . ." He reaches for something that feels true. "It's like they're being—poisoned—but they don't realize it. Even if they don't know about it, it's still happening. And it's not right, Maureen. It's just . . . mean."

She shakes her head. "You're being ridiculous."

"It's not ridiculous."

"It's not?" She considers him. "Why care about this now, Justin? You never did before."

"That's not true. I've always cared. You do too." Words so meaningless he's surprised they can be said. "Look," he says, "I love you, but doing this isn't right—"

"And leaving the one you love is right?"

"Sometimes. Yes."

"Have you found somebody else?"

"No!" He's startled. "No. Only you."

She nods, looks down at her dinner. She prods the peas with her fork, pushing a stray back to the herd. Justin watches a smile come to her face, and grow. She looks up and says, "You won't be able to leave. You'll start thinking about me. Me, sleeping beside someone who isn't you."

"I think about that all the time," he answers; and he does. "Look, I love you," he says again, and it sounds like a concession this time, a kind of bargaining. "But we need to think of your husband and child. That's all there is to it, Maureen."

"Really? I thought there was you and me."

"There is. But some things just can't happen."

The woman sighs; her gaze moves over the sideboard, the drinks cabinet, the archway, returns to him. "So you love me, but not my situation."

He tries, "I make things difficult for you."

"But if things were different, you would have stayed?"

"Yes—probably, yes—"

"Then we'll *make* things different. It's easy enough. You and I will stay the same, and everything else can change."

Something in Justin springs from its seat shrieking. "Maureen, we can't. We just can't. I should go. I'm sorry—"

"Justin, no, sit down! You haven't finished your dinner!"

But he's already pushing out his chair, he won't be stopped again. "I'm sorry, Maureen," he repeats, "but I can't."

He leaves her at the dinner table, steam roiling up from the meals. Through the house, down the driveway, to the footpath, across the lawn: he goes leaving nothing in his wake but a fast-flying kind of relief.

At home the television is burbling behind the closed door of the den. Justin changes out of his good clothes, then trots downstairs again. David and Plum are slumped on the couch watching a talent quest. They look up at him,

David sleepy-eyed. Justin asks, "What time is *Rosemary's Baby* on?"

"Are you going to watch it with me?" Plum struggles upright with hope.

"Maybe. Where's Mums and Fa?"

"They went for a walk," says David, and Plum nods. It is a typically inconvenient thing for his parents to do, right at this moment when Justin needs to get David out of the house before Maureen uses the child as an excuse to come to the door. He has no option but to tell Plum, "The lights are on next door. Mrs. Wilks must be home. You should take David back now. Then we won't be interrupted during the film."

Nothing gives Plum more joy than to watch movies in the dark with her brother. "Home time, Davy!" She chivvies the boy from his seat. Justin drops into the space they vacate, and as the girl and the child shamble from the room the thing that's clearest in his mind is a thankfulness that Cydar wasn't here to see it happen.

The cutlery is heavy. She had not wanted heavy cutlery, but there it is, this weight. The heaviness is all there is — after he left the room, there was nothing to see; after the front door closed, there was nothing to hear. She sits before the plates of unfinished food, the bottle of wine and the half-filled glasses, the pepper grinder and the single lily, and all of it is like a backdrop that can be rolled up or thrown away. Finally she puts the knife aside, and pats her cheeks, smooths her eyebrows, straightens her clothes. She sees, then, the pink petals and lime stem of the flower. She sees that the apricot sauce has lost its sheen. "Waste," she says; and rather than flowing into the room, the word ducks back inside her throat, causing her breathing to hitch. Her fingers are weaving between each other, and her hands feel wintry. Long ago, a palm reader had told her that her father would die unexpectedly, that she would have four sons, that she would know hard times financially, that in middle age she'd have problems with her heart. A life so unremarkable that Maureen had jokingly replied that she might as well lock herself inside the average garage and start the average car.

"You have to be somewhere and live somehow and do something and be someone," her mother always told her. "What's wrong with what you are?"

But her mother is satisfied with smallness. Ordinary is enough for her. She has never had high expectations in terms of happiness, achievement, depth of thought. Maureen, who can think of so much that's depressing, can't think of anything worse. To live like something taken from the shelf of a cut-price variety store.

The chicken is inedible, its sauce is glue. There's a trifle in the refrigerator — in the morning she will dig a hole and upend the dessert into it. The sponge and cream hitting the soil will make the sound of a monster.

When her mind goes to Justin, Maureen meets a whiteness that expands never-endingly.

She returns to thinking, instead, of her mother. Her mother is the sort of woman who says, "Be glad you have your health." Her mother can't see that life can be a boat on sapphire waters, a wild wind-trammeled cliff, the sleeper carriage of a transcontinental train, murder-suicides and reunions in the rain. That even a failure to be healthy can be a beautiful thing. If her mother were here, she would say, "It's better this way. You're a silly girl, Maureen." And if Maureen were to explain that Justin is a wind-trammeled cliff, her mother would scoff. *Silly girl.*

Maureen begins crying, one tear at a time. The tears drop from her jaw and spatter the gold-rimmed edge of the plate.

The knock on the door startles her, yanks her out of her chair; she is up and moving instantly, she's flying down the hall. The house is an indecipherable maze, the door torturously far away. "Wait!" she whimpers, terrified she won't reach it before he disappears. She wrenches the handle and pulls the door, and the sight of Plum and David is inexpressibly cruel, her hands flutter up in fear that she'll be sick. "Darlings!" she cries. "Come inside! Has it been raining? Have you had a lovely night? Has David been behaving? Have you had a lovely night?"

She backs down the hall with her son in her arms, her mind a runaway horse. The girl must not ask questions, she mustn't see the dining table. There cannot be silence, or Maureen will disintegrate. She chatters all the way down the hall, David sagging against her shoulder, ice-creamed face on the spotless jumpsuit. In the nursery Maureen lays the boy on the bed and tucks the blankets around him. "Wait," she says, "let me get you some money," and darts from the room leaving the girl beside the child, and skitters down the hall.

In the kitchen she clutches her stomach, gouging at the soft flesh there.

Her head is already hurting when she returns to the nursery. Plum is fiddling with the Smurfs that squat along the windowsill. "Aren't they awful?" Maureen says. "Bernie buys them for him. Such ugly little things. So what did you two do together? Did you have a nice time?"

"We watched television—"

"And how are your ears? Have you been using the methylated spirit? Show me—no, wait, just stand there a moment. Something about you looks different." Maureen cocks her head, brows tensing. "Aria, I think you've lost weight!"

The girl is thrilled. "Really? Really?"

"I'm not joking! You have! I told you you would, didn't I? Come here, let me hug you!"

And the knowledge that Plum is not the hugging kind makes infinitely more satisfying the fact that she flings herself without hesitation into Maureen's arms. They embrace deliriously, noses pressed against each other, Plum the padded totem pole, Maureen bony as a goat. "I'm going to buy you an outfit to wear at your party," Maureen promises, holding on to Plum tight. "You deserve something pretty, you wonderful girl! I'm so glad we've become friends! Aren't you?"

Later that night she'll remember this moment, and wonder if she's ever hated anyone more.

THE FINAL WEEK OF PLUM'S YEAR is golden. It reminds her of a fairground ride she's seen in black-and-white movies, where a swan-shaped boat glides through a tunnel on submerged tracks. She would like every day of her life to be lived inside a cup-like swan that knew where it was going, and where it would end.

The weather, of a sudden, loses its brashness; the north wind stops blowing, the sun retreats, and summer is finally done. Plum's school dress stops catching on patches of sweat, her armpits aren't muggy as tea. Her stomach is used to deprivation now, and no longer writhes noisily; when Caroline asks, "Where's your lunch gone, Plummy?" she's confident enough to say, "You don't need three meals a day.

Lunch is why people are fat." And her friends ogle her, and she feels the bread turn to sand in their mouths.

Classes are good; she does well in a math test; the Youth Group leader had sat beside Rachael at the meeting on Saturday night, so the friends have something over which to thrall. When Rachael had told him she'd miss the next meeting because of a friend's slumber party, the leader had answered, "That's no good," and there's much to discuss about *how* he'd said it, whether sadly or indifferently. "I think it sounds like he was disappointed," Plum generously tells her friend. In recognition of the approaching birthday, the girls treat Plum with deference in small ways. They laugh at her jokes and collect her rubbish with their own. On Wednesday, Rachael, Samantha and Dash announce that they've bought the present toward which they'd clubbed their money. "You'll love it," Samantha promises; "You need it," says Dash.

If none of them is curious as to the state of her ears, it's a silence that Plum welcomes. Now that the swelling has nearly subsided and the pain almost gone, it's embarrassing to recall how close she'd come to failing to be a girl with pierced ears. Twice a day she sluices her lobes with methylated spirit before feeding the blunt end of a needle into the holes to keep the piercings open. When she recollects the scarlet agony of infection, it's easy to believe there's something miraculous in her recovery. Maureen, like a nun, had divined what to do.

Plum starts dabbing methylated spirit on other parts of

her body that need fixing, and goes to bed each night feeling slightly parched.

The Datsun Skyline is in the Wilks driveway on Monday and Tuesday nights, but both evenings Maureen comes out into the garden and waves at Plum in her window. "David keeps talking about you, Rapunzel. Every day he asks, *Where's Aria?*" The thought makes a proud feeling bloom inside Plum, brings a loopy smile to her face. The same thing happens on Thursday when Maureen sings the birthday song to her, David mumbling several words behind. It is the eve of Plum's birthday and they are sitting at the counter in Maureen's kitchen, and in Plum's hand is a purple velvet box containing Maureen's present to her: a pair of silver earrings sporting the sparkle of two tiny but genuine diamonds, the receiving of which had rendered Plum teary. After the cake is cut there is a second gift, which Maureen fetches from her bedroom. It's a cornflower-blue, elastic-waisted dress, with no straps to hold the top half up, only another line of elastic that clings perilously to Plum's underarms when she tries on the garment in the bathroom. She stares at herself in the mirror, sees a strong-looking girl with black hair thick as horsetail falling to her bare shoulders. Partway down her arms begins what remains of her tan, and the piece of her chest that is exposed by the dress is pallid and spotty. "Don't worry about that," Maureen reassures her, and shows Plum how to use makeup to disguise the piebalding. From her cupboard Maureen takes a pair of strappy silver sandals, and somehow these Cinderella shoes harness Plum's ugly-sister feet. Her hair is brushed, lip gloss is applied, the earrings are pushed into place. "Stand up straight, shoulders back, nice cheery smile." Plum gazes at her image, breathing shallowly. The sandals, the dress, the diamonds in her ears seem to quiet the bleat that her heart has been making for months. She's seeing, in the mirror, the bird inside the box. She looks up at Maureen, face pinched with emotion. Maureen chuckles: "Shush, you deserve it. You're worth more than you think, Aria."

When Plum wakes the next morning, there's a large square present sitting on the end of her bed. Although diamonds could easily throw all other gifts into the shade, Plum is delighted with the roller skates her parents have given her, two smart white leather boots sporting chunky red wheels. In pajamas and dressing gown she tries on the skates; wobbles tectonically across the floor of the bedroom; takes them off again.

The day passes like a dream. Everyone is kind to her, as if a relative is dead. Her friends sing the birthday song when they gather under the tree. At dinner that night, Justin gives her a big paperback called *The Films of George Romero*. Inside are dozens of black-and-white photographs of the living dead. Cydar says callously, "I haven't had time to buy anything, sorry." Plum is hurt, but manages to stuff it down. She's too clever to spoil her day, or, worse, her tomorrow.

What she does do — because she's fourteen, because the redness is cured, because she has diamonds in the pocket of her cargo pants—is reveal to her family the fact of her pierced ears. Her brothers and parents crane across the table to get a better look. "Cool," says Justin. "What's done is done," says Fa. "They're your ears, I suppose," Mums tells her. Cydar sits back against the pew, turns the purple jewel box to the light. "Are these real?" he asks. "Why would she buy you diamonds?"

The smile falters on Plum's face. "I don't know. She's my friend."

"My friends don't give me diamonds."

"It's too much, isn't it?" realizes Fa.

Plum chews her lip, feels something recoil inside. By rights she should rush to Maureen's defense—Maureen who understands her, who respects her opinions, never treats her like a baby, doesn't laugh off and forget what Plum says—yet oddly her instinct is to conceal her instead. "I have a new dress too," she says. "A blue one. I bought it with my babysitting money. I saved up." And no one queries this, or possibly even hears. The earrings are passed across the table to Justin, who considers them impassively and remarks, "At least they're something you can pawn."

Plum retires early that night, having spent some time alone with the briefcase, holding each item in her hands. Rattled by the questioning of the diamonds and the lie about the dress, she requests of the objects, "Share your strength, share your strength. Today and tomorrow, share your strength." And although she does indeed feel some strength moving through her like soup, it's only when

Maureen comes into the garden, and Plum sees her lovely face and hears her reassuring voice, that her certainty returns, brawny as concrete — as if Maureen is a thousand times more powerful than the objects, and all that Plum really needs.

She goes to bed cleansed, having smeared methylated spirit on the marred parts of her body. Her bed has fresh sheets on it; in the corner, where she can see them, sit the roller skates and *The Films of George Romero*. Balled in her blankets, Plum is cozy with the sense that things have finally become good. Thirteen and all its bad luck is behind her. Fourteen will be the best.

Her guests arrive at four o'clock. Bowls of Twisties and Maltesers are waiting for them in the den. Sophie's gift is a little carousel. When a knob is turned, the skewered horses parade and a tinny "Edelweiss" plays. Victoria gives a fountain pen, which feels too classy for anything Plum would write. Caroline gives her an umbrella printed with quavers and treble clefs. Plum does not mention that she already owns an umbrella. The girls sit in the den, trying on Plum's earrings and admiring the new dress, stroking the crimps baked into Victoria's snowy hair. They talk about the essays they're working on, the nuisance of younger siblings, and whether or not Plum should be ashamed about the antique furniture. But all this is only killing time, and nothing important is said. They know they are waiting for

Rachael, Samantha and Dash. Until these arrive, the party can't begin.

They knock on the door just as Plum is starting to feel stretched and panicky. "It's Dash's fault!" caws Samantha, and Dash says, "It's Sam's fault!" The gift in Rachael's hands attracts buzzing attention: no present has ever been the wellspring of so much plotting and whispering. When it's passed into Plum's ownership the girls gather around the coffee table, shuffling close on their knees. The gift is small, as bumpy as a criminal's cranium, and the wrapping paper is not secondhand and creased from another present, but crisp and new. Plum peels the tape off carefully as the friends exchange lightning glances. "What is it?" asks Caroline, as though it's obvious to everyone but her. "Shut up," says Samantha. "Just watch." Plum folds back the paper, and there, lying in the cup of golden wrapping, is a tube of mascara, a pot of blue eyeshadow, a compact of blusher and a canister of lipstick. "Wow!" Plum lifts a pleased face. "Thanks!"

"It's for when you're a model." Samantha smiles creamily.

"Told you you'd need it," says Dash.

"We thought you could start practicing now—"

"Even though you're already such a goddess," injects Dash.

"—and then, when you're in magazines, you'll remember us."

"Rach! Aria will be too famous to remember us!"

The smile clings leech-like to Plum's face. She cannot let it fall. The merest hint of weakness will begin the unraveling of the day. She knows how to lessen the impact of hurt: pretend it isn't happening, that the words aren't said and the deed not done. "Thanks," she says again, and when her hand closes around them the cosmetics knock together as richly as yachts. "That's great."

"That's mean." Caroline looks across the coffee table at Rachael, Samantha and Dash. "You're mean."

"It's not mean," corrects Plum. "It's great."

Samantha plucks the lipstick out of Plum's fist, pulls the cap with a pop. "If Aria's going to be a model, she better start practicing now. Pucker, Aria."

So Plum, on her knees, is forced to make a ridiculous face, her mouth a tight circle while the lipstick is scuffed from lip to lip. The cosmetic feels like wet soil as it's applied, and smells reptilian. Although the process is quicker and without pain, it is strangely worse than her ears. There's nothing about it that is courageous, there's only Samantha's gigantic fingers and Plum's cravenness, and the silence that descends on the five witnesses. There is her party, already spoiled, and the realization that, at fourteen, nothing will change. She won't tell Samantha that, this close, her face is as hairy as a fly's; she won't squeeze the lipstick like butter in a fist, or jump to furious feet. She will let them treat her how they like, because the alternative is worse. "There," says Samantha. "How's that?"

Sophie tips her head. "Oh, she looks pretty."

"She does!" Victoria laughs marvelously. "Aria, you do!"

"It doesn't look super-good," Dash tells Plum.

"I think it does," says Caroline. "You look like a model, Aria."

The door opens, and the friends look up like daisies: but it is only Mums wheeling in the drinks table, on which sits a vat of ginger-beer punch. "Hello Mrs. Coyle," chorus Samantha, Rachael and Dash. "Thank you for having us." They help themselves to scoops of punch while Mums tops up the Twisties bowl. Plum sees her notice the lipstick on her daughter's mouth, sees her keep the observation to herself. As soon as the door closes and Mums is gone, Samantha asks like a whipcrack, "Are your brothers home?"

"Cydar is. He's in his bungalow. Justin is at work." Plum had been aghast when he'd driven off that morning, though he'd promised and vowed and sworn to be home in time for dinner. She has walked near the park, and his car wasn't there, which has given her hope that he has told the truth. "He'll be here later."

Rachael elbows Caroline. "Caz wants to marry Justin."

The pale girl shies backward. "I don't! As *if* I do!"

"You do! You said you do! You want to have a wedding cake with a little plastic Justin and a little plastic Caz. And you and Aria can be sisters-in-law —"

"Sammy! Shut up! All I said was that he looks like a nice husband!"

"Yeah — *your* nice husband!"

"How do *you* know what a nice husband looks like?"

Caroline flails. "You can tell! You can! It's that look, like he'd paint the house—"

"Paint the house!" The words force the friends to the floor, six dissolving witches. They laugh because they're sure they know everything able to be known and life holds no further mystery for them, not even about things they haven't yet known and will not know for years—first touch, first defeat, nights shared, days forgotten, mistakes made, words unsaid, the saying of too many words. The heaviness of success, the gray valleys of loss, the clay feet of love, the greediness of time. Plum laughs because she can, it is so extremely funny; and because when they're laughing at Caroline they are not laughing at her. Yet deep inside, a knot of disquiet ties up in her. Justin won't marry Caroline—but other things will happen, and they will make Plum's life, and Plum will have little choice about some of them, and no choice at all in many. She claws at the flank of an armchair, feeble with laughter; but life has turned to look over its shoulder at her, and life has the look of a dragon. When no one is watching she drags her wrist across her tacky lips.

They lie for a while side-by-side on the floor, beached on their unrolled sleeping bags, talking about songs and the lead singers of bands, about teachers and which ones have been made to cry, about the state-school boys who throw the private-school girls' bags onto the tracks at train stations. They talk, of course, about Rachael's Youth Group leader, whom some of the friends are beginning to hate.

"This is boring," Samantha says suddenly; and they all recognize it then, as if boredom has a bad smell, and Plum is mortified. "Let's go to your room, Aria. We'll do some more modeling."

Plum must clamber to her feet. "OK!"

Noisily they carry their glasses of punch and the bowl of Twisties upstairs. Plum's bedroom is large, but the seven girls seem to fill every inch of it — they bump against the furniture, reach for the same item, squeeze past one another to look out the window. Their voices collide like clashing colors, crowd like balloons against the ceiling. Everything Plum owns is exposed to their slab-sided scrutiny. When she was young, last year, last month, Plum had loved showing off her bedroom to her friends; now, hedged into a corner as her clothes are inspected and the radio turned on, as her porcelain cats are tortured and the photographs turned to where the light will fade them and the teddy bears are made to attack, she feels awful, strangulated. This room is *her,* her one place in the whole world: but, "What's this?" her friends are asking, demanding as seagulls. "Where'd you get it? How much was it? Why did you choose that color? What's so good about that? Can I have this? I had one of these. It broke, so I threw it away." And because defending the toys and the record albums and the brand-new jeans and her first pair of baby shoes would dangerously expose their preciousness, Plum can only stand in the corner, apologizing and disowning, barely coherent and grinning.

Samantha's big head is in the cupboard. "You don't wear peasant skirts, do you? They make your bum look huge, you know. Before you buy clothes, Aria, you should ask my advice."

Victoria is tilting novels out from the shelves. "Can I borrow one of these? Or all of them? I've got nothing to read."

Rachael is peering into the mirror, dotting Plum's acne cream on her spots. "I've tried this stuff before," she says. "It doesn't work."

Caroline is sprawled across the bed. "You've had that poster of kittens since you were little, haven't you, Aria?"

"Only a few years." The elastic around the bib of Plum's dress is beginning to feel tight. When she shifts it, she sees it has carved a blazing line into her flesh. "Since I was ten."

"Probably time to take it down," says Dash. "Kittens!"

Sophie is trying on the roller skates, tightening the white laces at her ankles. Everyone knows Sophie can ice-skate and ride horses, and learned gymnastics for seven years. The skates fit her perfectly, and she stands and spins about. "Can I take them outside?"

"OK!" The word bumps up, lurching Plum from the wall. "Hey, everyone, that's a good idea, let's take the skates outside—"

"Shh!" says Victoria. "Listen!"

Like a herd of deer they lift their heads and look toward the door. There's a man's voice laughing somewhere below them; suddenly, a man's feet coming up the stairs. It is

Justin, home. The girls swivel to Caroline: "Now's your chance!" Samantha hisses. "He's here, you can ask him! Wedding bells, wedding bells!" And Caroline, yowling with terror, drops from the bed and scrambles underneath it even as Justin appears in the doorway, as tousled and vital as an Olympian. His elegant face, his long legs, his twinkling eyes and baby-sweet smile eclipse completely the ugly bottle-shop polo shirt with its gallivanting bottle of beer. "Hello," he says, and the appeal he radiates could loosen planets from their rotations. "Hi, old Plummy."

"Hi Justin." The friends hunker into themselves. Plum says, "Hi," so casually.

Her brother slouches in the doorway, nudges a lock of hair from his eyes. "What's been happening?"

"None of your business. We're taking the skates outside."

"Ah." He glances around, and Plum realizes that he's lost for words, is swamped with panic on his behalf. Then he notices the roller skates on Sophie's feet, and, in a moment that scores into Plum's heart unforgettably, he says, "Be careful, Soph. You could break yourself on those things."

It's like a slap with a rose: everyone is jealously and absolutely stunned not by the fact that he so clearly knows her name but that he actually *shortened* it. Sophie, red in the cheeks, mumbles, "I'll try not to."

"Good." Justin searches the forest of staring faces for his sister. "So everything's fine? Anything I can do?"

"No." Plum has regained a cocky equilibrium —

indeed, she's soaring. Probably nothing in the world is as wonderful as Justin. "You can go away, that's what. Shoo."

"All right. But I'll be coming back later for birthday cake, remember."

"Bye, Justin." Her friends are a zombie chorus, immobile while they listen to him walk down the hall. Plum teeters, destabilized by reflected glory. Samantha turns and asks almost pleadingly, "Does he have a girlfriend?"

Dash gasps at the audacity. "I don't think he'd like *you*—"

"Shut up, Dash, I'm only *asking*—"

"Lots of girls like him," says Plum solemnly.

Caroline's legs are kicking as she caterpillars out from under the bed—Victoria jumps sideways to avoid a flying foot. Gathering her limbs she sits up, blinking and splotched with dust. "Your husband's gone," Rachael tells her, "but he's coming back later for birthday cake."

Caroline, though, is looking at Plum. She unfurls a spidery hand and asks, "Plummy, what's this?"

Later Plum will wonder why she didn't hear the familiar *chock chock* of the briefcase latches springing open. While Justin had lounged in the doorway, the whole room had seemed to roar—but not so loudly that she shouldn't have heard the sound of the coming catastrophe. Perhaps a warning would have made no difference, or even made things worse; but how fragile *power* must have been, how feeble must have been *happiness,* to have disintegrated so inaudibly, like crumbs dropped from a height.

In Caroline's hand is the Fanta yo-yo. Its clam-like orange shell is as virulent as a fire alarm. Caroline had forsaken a small hill of chocolate to buy this thing which would be a lasting memento of a day at the Show. How proud she had been of making that choice. Often Plum has held the yo-yo to her lips, willing into its coiled string the words, *The choices I make will be the choices you make. I am important to you.* The dear yo-yo, the most humble of the objects: looking back, she would never have guessed that the *yo-yo* would be the one to betray her.

Plum's heart starts to beat sickeningly. Her only choice is to brazen it out. "It's a yo-yo, Caz."

"But — it's *my* yo-yo, isn't it?"

". . . No, it's mine. It's just a dumb yo-yo."

Caroline frowns, not angrily. "But it *looks* like my yo-yo. My yo-yo's lost. I've been looking for it for ages."

"It's just a stupid yo-yo!" Plum says it too vehemently into the silenced room. Her friends are watching her, their eyes cold stones. Pushed into the corner Plum says, "You're not the only person who has a yo-yo, Caz. All yo-yos look the same —"

"Then what's this?"

The girl on the floor opens her other arachnid hand, and in her palm is a tangle of silver links and tiny trinkets, a handbag, a heart, a trumpet. "Oh!" The word oofs out of Sophie, who staggers forward, weighted by the skates. "My charm bracelet! Plum — where did you find it?" And Plum, elbows against the wall, takes a final terrified glance at her, this girl she's liked and admired and even secretly loved a little, knowing she'll never again see the delight that's spilling over her face.

"Find it!" It is Rachael who is fastest at adding up a lost yo-yo and a lost bracelet and a hiding place under a bed. "She didn't *find* it — she stole it! You stole Sophie's bracelet, didn't you, Plum? You stole Caz's yo-yo!"

The accusation is so savage that Sophie steps backward with shock. "No!" Plum barks hotly. "I wouldn't! As *if* I would! I *found* that bracelet —"

"Yeah? Where? In Sophie's bedroom? On the day we pierced your ears?" Understanding arrives brightly in Rachael's eyes. "That's right, isn't it? You stole the bracelet when we left you in Sophie's bedroom, after we pierced your ears."

"Oh my God," says Dash.

"You slag," whispers Samantha.

"I didn't!" Plum writhes. "Why would I? I found it at school, in the quadrangle, I didn't even *know* it was Sophie's —"

Victoria pipes up wanly from where she's huddled at the bookcase. "Don't say she's stealing if she isn't, Rach."

"But this *is* my yo-yo." Caroline sounds amazed. "I recognize this scratch. I dropped it on the road and it got this scratch . . ."

The six girls stare at Plum then, who is packed into the corner and whose teeth are bared in fear. In the silence they hear the ginger punch defizzing in the glasses. Caroline says, "Why didn't you just *say* you wanted my yo-yo, Plum? I would have given it to you."

Samantha asks, "What else have you stolen, bitch?"

"I didn't steal anything!" The words rip from Plum—wildness is all that's left to her. "This is stupid! You're being stupid!"

Caroline looks at Samantha. "There's a whole box of things under the bed."

Plum cries out like a shot bird; Dash dives for the floor. The briefcase is pulled into the light, its unlockable lid thrown back. Plum lunges from the corner, to rescue her treasures or flee, she's not sure: but Samantha's bulk blocks her, and she digs into the corner again. Later she'll be struck by how meager the objects had looked, lying there in their beds of silk and cotton ball. Such gewgaws could never have given her what she needs, she should have known they would leave her falling, with nothing to break her fall. "My watch!" bawls Rachael; "My necklace!" screams Victoria. The wristwatch and jade pendant are brandished in the air. Samantha plucks up the ancient coin with a derisive snort. Dash holds the Abba badge between two fingertips. Plum's heart hitches to see Sophie reach out for the glass lamb. Held to the light, the lamb sparkles for Sophie just as it sparkled for Plum. "My grandmother gave me this," Sophie whispers. "I've looked for it everywhere. I thought Mum had sucked it up in the vacuum cleaner."

"Plum," says Victoria, "how could you?"

"Why?" Caroline asks forlornly. "*Why* would you?"

Plum turns her eyes to the blankness of the floor. Her face is flaming and she would like to spurt a fountain of tears, but the weeping won't come. Underneath her agony, she is dry and cold. What must happen will happen: but they cannot force her to explain. "It's just junk," she says thickly. "You didn't need it."

"So *what* if we didn't need it? That doesn't mean you could *steal* it."

Victoria rests her head against the wall. "I didn't need this necklace. I still liked it, though."

"Same with this coin," Samantha says. "I don't *need* it. But I still want it. It's *mine*."

"You stole a bit of each of us." Sophie frowns down at the lamb. She's reaching for a reason *why,* but the answer keeps winnowing away. Rachael announces the only fact that is brutally obvious: "You're a thief, Aria. You're a thieving bitch."

Plum cringes in her corner. "I was going to give it back," she tries, but it's a lie as thin as water, and the words drain away. Sophie takes a gulp of distress, sits down to unlace the roller skates. Rachael's baleful gaze stays on Plum as friendships are severed and withdrawn. "This watch belonged to my mother," she says. "It's an *heirloom.* I lost it the day I broke my arm. You found it — and you were going to keep it. You didn't care that I was sad about losing it. You didn't care about any of us."

"That's not true," Plum moans, but Rachael snaps back,

"Yes it is. You're disgusting, Aria, Plum, whatever your name is."

"And creepy," says Dash. "Keeping our stuff in a coffin under her bed."

"She makes me sick," says Samantha.

Rachael slips the watch into a pocket, looks around at her friends. "I don't want to stay here," she says. "I'm going home."

"Me too." Samantha and Dash declare it together; Victoria agrees quickly, "Me too."

Caroline climbs to her feet, says, "I wish you hadn't done it, Plummy."

Only Sophie says nothing, and does not look at Plum.

"No—listen—wait!" Plum stumbles back to life, recognizing this is the moment to make the final protest: but she is just a doll now, empty and half-alive. Her words are scraps of nothingness that catch on the balustrade as she follows her friends down the stairs. "I'm not like that, that's not true, you don't understand." None of it means anything, and it's a relief when Samantha, reaching the front door, wheels to spit, "Get away from us."

"What about our sleeping bags?" frets Caroline.

Rachael says, "Roll up our sleeping bags and leave them outside. My dad will come and get them."

"What a great party!" Dash laughs.

"She makes me sick," reiterates Samantha.

The six girls in their party clothes herd each other down the veranda steps and across the patchy lawn. Not even

Caroline glances back to where Plum stands at the door. When her friends have marched out of sight, Plum's gaze begins a slow journey through the trees, across the gardens, along brick fences and thin power-lines. The evening sky is still blue, but dusk has dirtied its hem. It's the time of day for boiling water, feeding children, switching on the television, shutting windows and closing doors. Soon Mums will call out to say that the vol-au-vents are ready, having delivered them on a platter to the den.

Everything has been decimated, but for now the house is peaceful. Plum turns on her silver-sandaled heels and climbs the stairs to her bedroom. The room seems unusually quiet, and bigger than normal, the walls untypically high. The air inside it is tanged with the odor of ginger beer. The briefcase is lying where Rachael kicked it, half-hidden under the bed. Cotton balls tumble over its sides. Plum gets stiffly to her knees, tucks the padding back into place, closes the lid and secures the catches, and slides the case into the darkness.

From along the hallway she can hear the drumming of water: Justin is taking a shower. Downstairs, in the kitchen, Fa will be laying out napkins and mismatched cutlery. Mums will be reading the cooking instructions printed on a box brittle with frost from the freezer. Outside, in his bungalow, Cydar will be leaning back in his chair, stretching his arms to the ceiling.

Plum perches carefully on the edge of her bed, and wonders how to make herself die.

ᴘᴇ CYDAR SITS ON THE BUNGALOW STEP, a cigarette between two knuckles, sitting like a folded bird so his kneecaps touch his chest and his toes hook the tread. Between the bungalow and the house tall trees rise randomly, weeds smother rockeries, shrubs straggle across paths. Earthen trails weave through a wilderness of privet and geranium, linking house to clothesline to shed to side gate; there's a broad bowl in the dirt that was once a pond, or the idea of a pond, where Cydar might have raised spotted koi but instead is the site of a forest of thistle. There are no gardeners in the Coyle family, and what interference the plants receive occurs when storms break a branch from a husky gum or the plumber comes to dig into the old pipes, uncovering as he does so small items lost for decades.

Plastic soldiers, metal cars, the crumbling bladder of a football. Autonomy should make the garden serene, but Cydar knows enough about the nature of life to understand that every living thing is a battlefield.

Beneath the clothesline with its network of baggy wires, lurking around the door like a dog hoping to come inside, is an area of lawn that Justin keeps mown, a sea-green breaker between civilization and the wild. Across this field is hopping a troupe of sparrows. The fat little creatures must be acquaintances, possibly friends: yet they squabble and bully, flee and pursue. One small bird pecks at a hub of garlic bread the way a sculptor taps at stone, wiping his beak intermittently on the ground between his toes; others are investigating Cheezels, picking flakes of pastry from the grass. Mums has thrown out the uneaten food from Plum's party, and the birds skitter amid a flotsam of popcorn, potato chips, hot dogs, bread rolls. An hour earlier, just as he'd finished tamping down the papers of a joint, Cydar had watched his mother step sideways out the back door, the pile of leftovers heaped in her arms. She'd stood on the lawn upending bags and boxes, shaking their contents to the ground. Frozen pies and sausage rolls had bounced away. His mother had crushed the empty boxes with her feet, and stood for a time staring at nothing. Then, as Cydar had struck a match, she'd noticed her son watching her. She had waved a hand at the strewn bounty, looked helplessly across at him. "What else could I do?" she'd asked.

The sight of the party food had become oppressive. His

mother hates waste, but opening the freezer should not be so depressing. So, "Nothing," Cydar had answered. *We are incapable of doing anything more than this.* He'd proffered the joint, and instead of frowning and telling him off, his mother had just shaken her head.

And now, an hour later, most of the food is gone, and Cydar wishes that the worst of life was like this, something that could be pecked away by tiny birds and converted into flight.

He had stepped into the house, on the night of his sister's party, expecting the kitchen to be nightmarish with adolescent girls, their jostling and volume and vanity. He'd expected to see Mums by the oven, swearing under her breath, hot dogs surging in a pot of boiling water. There should have been a mountain range of wrapping paper, gifts lined up on the sideboard, birthday cards slipping off the mantel. This is how it has been at all Plum's parties past. Instead there had been silence, and the pot of water on the stove was flatly cold and clear. Cydar had not thought to worry, however, because the silence and the emptiness hadn't seemed dire, only unexpected; he hadn't thought to be apprehensive, only displeased to have closed his textbooks before the necessary time. When he found Justin and Mums and Fa in the hall, he'd asked, "What's going on? Is dinner ready?"

"Her guests have gone." Mums had whispered it, as if *gone* meant *deceased.* Cydar had misunderstood: "What?"

"Plum's friends walked out of the party," Justin said.

"We think they've gone home," explained Fa. "We don't know why. Plum won't say."

And Cydar had felt it then, the dankness. Something had happened, the kind of happening that would never completely stop happening. Years from now, the four of them will be able to remember standing here, remember the compression in their chests. "Where is she?" he'd asked, his first instinct being to see her — not to question or to bolster her but just to check, as he'd once checked her in a hospital nursery thinking *hello hello hello.* Yet when told his sister was in her room and not saying anything beyond a few dull words — *they don't like me, they wanted to leave* — the instinct had released its grip. Cydar would not be someone she was forced to endure, he wouldn't come like a crow.

And he has kept to himself in the days since — all of the family has kept to itself, bottling down its dismay like a bad genie. They have watched Plum move around the house, sit at the table, switch on the TV, and no one has asked *what did happen?* They have found many things to talk about in her presence, and never about what happened. They've watched her hoist her socks, leave for school, do her homework, go to bed, they've heard in her voice a subduedness that was never there before: still no one has uttered a word. They can't save her, these parents and brothers who have never been able to save themselves. Any of them would gladly return happiness to her, if happiness were something lightweight and easy to retrieve, but it's a long time since anything beyond the rudimentary was within their reach. So Cydar spends hours at university, and Fa brings home Violet Crumbles for dessert, and Mums cooks the meals her daughter prefers, and Justin scans the guide for classic films. This is the best they can do.

Cydar sits forward, chin on his knee. Smoke weaves whitely through his hair. A sparrow pecks up a bud of popcorn and flies away, skipping over the paling fence and into the neighboring yard.

There'd been a knock at the front door on the night of the party, the disturbance sending volts through the air. Mums had hurried to answer it. Fa had turned down the television, and he and his sons had sat still and prick-eared. When they'd heard the pleasant purr, Justin's glance had swung to Cydar. There was nothing troubled in his look, only a cool annoyance. Mums returned, flopped into her chair, said, "It was Mrs. Wilks, from next door. Plum had invited her for cake. I told her the party was over. I didn't know what to say. But she seemed to know what I meant. *Girls can be unspeakable,* she said."

It's not *girls,* Cydar had wanted to retort: it's the *world.* Instead he'd reached out to turn up the volume of the television. Now, on the bungalow step, he adds, *Us, too.* We, who can't help her, as if she's made of stone, like us. Something other than just a child.

His chin is digging into his knee, but he doesn't straighten. He lifts the cigarette and smokes it down to the very stub. Curls of fringe come close to being burned;

smoke makes his eyes water. A magpie has arrived at the banquet now, forcing the sparrows away. Behind the birds rises the weathered house, its windows darkened and doors cheerlessly closed. Cydar's bungalow is refuge — his brother and parents find reason to visit, to stand before the priestly fish. Plum, however, hasn't come. She hasn't anything to confess to the fish, or to him. She can't form the words, as nobody can. If he could speak, Cydar would say, *Don't let them win.* Instead, unforgivably, nothing.

In the bushes close to the fence, behind the festering pile of vegetable shavings and the remains of last year's autumn leaves, an ice-cream cake is melting into the soil, slumping sludgily, bleeding chocolate sauce. Around its crawling edge a million ants have gathered to drink themselves into oblivion.

She is never hungry: for days she's had no desire to eat. She picks at dinner and breakfast, forcing her jaws to work. She is relieved when her lunch leaves her hand and thumps the bottom of the rubbish bin. She finds it difficult even to think, and what thoughts she has clog up in her head and fuse indecipherably. She doesn't want to talk to herself, inhabit herself, continue to be herself. If she could, she would shrug free of her body, and leave this mess behind.

The morning after the party Plum had woken in her bed, and the recollection of the previous day must have

been in her head waiting impatiently for her conscious-
ness to return, for it swooped down like an eagle, terrible
talons bared. It's a feeling she's grown accustomed to in
the days since; she walks in anguish, breathes it in, sighs it
out. She had telephoned Caroline that afternoon, chewing
her fingernails, prepared to be contrite and also defensive
if necessary, perhaps indignant over the spoiling of her
party. Caroline should have been the weakest, the most forgiving, the easiest to persuade. Instead she said, "Maybe
we shouldn't talk to each other, Plum. I don't care about
the yo-yo. But sometimes things aren't the same, don't
you reckon?"

"But listen Caz, I've been thinking, let's just you and
me be friends! We don't need those others, I've always liked
you the best anyway—"

"We *can* be friends," agreed Caroline: "We'll be secret
friends, OK? Because I still want to be friends with them.
But I'll be your secret friend . . ."

Plum had put the receiver in its cradle, returned to
her bedroom. She'd drawn the briefcase out from under
her bed, examined the lining and the cotton balls as if
something might have been missed: nothing had. She had
closed the lid and fastened the locks, and carried the briefcase downstairs to the junk cupboard and pushed it far
toward the back, where she wouldn't have to see it again.
Secret friend.

On Monday morning Plum had gone to school, because
the choice was to plead sickness for the rest of her life or to

tell Mums the reason why she didn't want to go. During the bus journey she had noticed the absence of something, some feeling she'd come to know: and what was gone was the bubble that's her home-self, her certain-self. The bubble didn't sink that morning, because it wasn't there to fall. Plum looked inside, and found it no longer existed. That piece of her was gone. She felt like someone living alone on a planet.

She'd expected rumor of the briefcase to have reached the school before she did — for Dash and Samantha to have caught an early train so every girl could hear the story before the ringing of the assembly bell. But in the corridors no one looked at her sideways or sniggered as she walked past. This could only mean that nobody knew. Plum wasn't so foolish as to hope it meant nobody would ever know. Rachael and Samantha and Dash would leak the scandal slowly, like poisonous fumes from the ground; and part of Plum was morbidly interested to see it happen. In the classrooms she had watched as the story flowed like a tide from girl to girl, passed inside notes, whispered into ears. Watching, she'd felt unusually and keenly alive, alive the way a knife is sharp, so the humiliation she was enduring was perfect, like the paring of skin from a hard apple.

At lunchtime Plum hadn't known what to do or where to go. She discovered it is difficult — it is almost impossible — to maintain the pretense of preoccupation for an hour. She knew that some girls were staring at her, following her with their words. Other girls neither stared nor cared, uninterested in her crimes and indifferent to her plight. Finally she found a concrete corner, far from the lawn with its graceful oak tree, littered with icy-pole sticks and chewing gum and cardboard, yet still a sanctuary: she had covered her face with her hands and cried, hot with anger and lank with suffering, and crying didn't console her but it did kill some time.

During the last lesson of the day, Geography, a girl had circled an arm around her pencil case as Plum walked past her desk. "Mine," the girl said, and there had been giggles and snorts. Plum had taken a desk in a corner, and no one sat beside her. She concentrated on the blue lines on her paper until they wavered and blurred. She thought about *The Village of the Damned* and *The Stepford Wives.* She thought about *Carrie,* and wished she was her.

The days that follow are the same—wretched, and much too long. Each morning Plum boards the bus hoping that this will be the day of reunion, that Tuesday will be the day of pity and Wednesday the day of remembrance and Thursday the day of irresistibility, but the week isn't like that at all. Rachael, Samantha and Dash don't look at her; it's clear that, to them, Plum doesn't and never will exist. Victoria and Sophie wear the faces of the recently bereaved: Plum no longer exists for them either, although she might be a ghost. Caroline sees her, but only once makes the mistake of smiling—then she's jerked to her senses so violently by Samantha that her scrawny neck almost breaks.

They do not need to worry, however. Plum doesn't try

to speak to them. All her energy is devoted to maintaining a force field around herself. The force field is not like the bubble had been — it does not rise and fall. It is permanently raised in an attempt to keep everything out. She dips her head in her locker when her friends walk by, she takes a seat among the misfits in the back rows of the classrooms. She draws no attention to herself by asking or answering questions. She lurks in the shadows during gym, wary of medicine balls coming toward her head. At lunchtime, she goes to the library. During recess, she hides. At home, she keeps her suffering to herself, bottled up in her hard cold glassy body, and does not ask for comfort. It is better that way.

But it's not better — nothing makes it better — and by Friday Plum is brittle with desperation. When she sees Sophie standing, unguarded, at the tail of the tuckshop line, she doesn't hesitate to duck into place behind her. "Hi," she says. "Buying a Wagon Wheel?" Because her old friend loves Wagon Wheels, it's a small sweet knowledge that links them.

Sophie turns, and looks at her. She doesn't smile, but she doesn't sneer. The tuckshop is in a corner of the undercroft, far from the brightness and swirling air of the open doors. In the gloom there's a kind of privacy, but Plum feels her vulnerability. "Did you see Dash's face?" she asks, and her voice is brassy, she has no practice at apologies. "She must really love Abba. She thinks she's so ace, but she loves Abba. What an idiot!"

"I like Abba," Sophie replies. "I love Abba."

"So do I!" Plum squeaks. "I had a T-shirt! When I was about eight, a yellow T-shirt with a picture of Abba, and *Abba* written on it in big purple letters. I meant—what I mean is—it was just a *badge*. It wasn't like an autograph or a record or something, it was only a badge, she loves a dumb *badge*—"

"Yes," says Sophie. "That's why you took it."

Plum lurches, the queue has moved forward, they can smell the calorific aroma of doughnuts and strawberry milk. "No, I didn't *take* it—well, I took it, but I was only *borrowing*. I was going to give everything back. I had this plan, it was a *game*—"

"A game!" Sophie's face crumples. "If you'd wanted to borrow my bracelet and the lamb, you could have asked. I would have said yes. But you didn't ask, you just *took,* without caring about me—*wanting* me to be sad!"

"No! No! It wasn't like that!"

"I *cried* about my bracelet, Plum! You *saw* me crying, and you just sat there, *pretending* to be my friend—"

"I *am* your friend!"

"Don't lie, Plum!" There is real fury in Sophie, Plum hadn't anticipated. "All you do is lie! You haven't even said *sorry*!"

"Sorry!" Plum yowls. "Sorry sorry sorry!"

"Shut up! You're not sorry!"

"I *am* sorry! Do you want me to say sorry or not?"

"I want you to *be* sorry—sorry for *stealing,* not for being *caught!*"

"I'm *sorry.*" She can't say it in a way that makes it sound sincere. Desperation makes her plead, "If *you* were a friend, you'd forgive me!"

Sophie answers, "I don't want to be your friend. You're a mean person, Plum. I thought you weren't, but you are."

"Rachael is meaner than me!" Plum protests. "Samantha is much meaner!"

Sophie stares at her; she gives a short, gusty laugh. "You're strange, aren't you," she says. "It's like you've got nothing inside."

And although they have reached the head of the queue now, with the tuckshop lady staring at them and a box of Choo Choo Bars right there at Sophie's elbow, the girl strides away without ordering, refusing to stand in Plum's rotten shade one moment more. She walks through the undercroft without looking back, heading for the open doors and the sunshine and the grass and the trees beyond.

Plum steps out of the queue, into a blissful darkness. Here is a place where light never reaches, where dust has gathered for decades; here she has almost vanished. She feels herself contracting until only her eyes are left large and open. Everywhere she looks she sees girls clustered in friendships like flowers—fields of flowers, and tidy posies, and dainty perfect pairings. All of them have somewhere to be, something to do, someone to talk to. But Plum is isolated, a writhing repulsive creature, and not one among these holy hundreds is obliged to make space for her. No explanation will redeem her. Begging is what she'd bow to, but it would not work.

She goes home that afternoon something other than what she's been.

Plum Coyle has never been very happy with herself—she's chumpish and she's awkward and there's something else wrong about her, some objectionable streak to her nature which means she'll never be popular, things will go askew, she'll frequently be misinterpreted. In her heart there are many admirable things, but it's hard for these to wriggle through her thick skin of obtuseness. She's tried and tried to be, for the world, the person she knows herself to be. She can't do it though, it's impossible. Time and again, that good person gets twisted about, or goes unrecognized. It's exhausting, and it hurts. Better, then, to stop exposing that fragile Plum to the dangerous light. Better to extinguish her completely, and become something steely and impervious, a ball bearing or a chunk of earth. The good Plum's loss would serve this world right; and it must be easier to live feeling nothing, as does a chunk of earth.

And the peculiar thing is: Plum is relieved. Deciding to feel nothing means she can stop trying to be something. It's a relief to turn off the force field, which has been draining her strength. Nothing doesn't need protection, because it cannot be harmed.

She knows that Mums and Fa and Justin and Cydar

will go on loving her anyway—they won't mind if she's a ball bearing. The thought of their affection makes Plum teary. From now on, she'll keep within the circle of her house and her parents and her brothers, and never care about anything beyond these, but live like a canary that's content in its cage or like that prim authoress who roamed the moors and hid in her room whenever company came to the rectory. She will follow the world's progress by watching TV, maybe get a telescope like Jimmy Stewart in *Rear Window*. This will be her, a stone in a lake, untouchable, unseen, undisturbed, and the prospect fills Plum not with loneliness, but with peace. Stretched out on her bed, she smiles up at the ceiling; for the first time all week, she's willing to live and breathe. It's luxury to think that she'll never be hurt again. She will have her family and her home and perhaps Maureen, and that will be enough.

But she can't tell about the briefcase and the unraveling of her party—not yet, and maybe never. Maybe one day when she's extremely old, too old to be ashamed, but not before. Her family would forgive her, and possibly understand; Justin and Cydar might even be amused. But for now Plum's disgrace is a howling thing, and she simply cannot. She hasn't opened her window all week, she has kept her bedroom door closed. She'd like to go down to the den and snuggle into her father's side, she'd like to lie on her neighbor's lawn and grow sleepy to the sound of Maureen. But, for now, it's easier to be alone. A single soft glance could still kill her.

SHE TAKES THE OPPORTUNITY. Justin is unlocking the door of his car and she's there, on the footpath: "Justin. Hello."

He looks up, across the roof of the Holden — she feels his gaze leap to her. A week hasn't changed him. He's still slim and somehow windswept, his hair falling in black curls and his watch loose around his wrist. The casual untidiness, she's always thought, of a riverbed. Yet the week has been long, like a slow sea journey, long enough for Maureen to fear he'll have forgotten the things that brought him back time and again; and in fact something catches in his voice when he says, "Hi. Maureen."

"Do you remember me?" This makes him smile, which is an answer she adores. "Going out?" she asks.

"Yeah," he says. "Nowhere interesting."

"That's where I'm going. Nowhere interesting." She is holding a cream envelope, as on the first day they met, and she waves it at him. She would like to take his hand and, knowing what she knows now, lead him back to that very first day. A week of reflection has made her see that they have been too tentative, allowing themselves to be hindered by elements that aren't really obstacles at all. The best way is to be forthright from the start—to craft him into who she wants him to be while he is still blind, as men always go blind. If she'd done so, she would not be standing where the footpath meets the Coyle driveway in a line that she's unable to cross. Serves herself right; but nothing is irretrievably lost, and she won't make errors again. "I've missed you," she tells him.

Justin shifts his weight. "Well, I've missed you."

"It seems an eternity."

"Well," he says again, "it's a week."

"A week!" She raises her arms in exasperation, the envelope flying up like a dove. She tucks away for later contemplation the fact that he knows the number of days. "Every time there was a footstep, I thought it was you."

He smiles slightly. "No."

"Oh, I know! I felt very teased. I think David thought I'd gone mad. Maybe I have." She gives a small shudder to illustrate. Her voice is loud, her grin wide, standing here on the footpath she feels as exposed as a mannequin, but she *cannot* cross the line and go to him, yet nor is she willing to turn and leave . . . It has rained in the night, and the path is stained with greasy plates of damp, the melaleuca in the naturestrip still dripping. It's not cold, but it is possible to detect a coming thinness in the weather, a veil brushing the skin. She hugs herself against this, and against the flatness of his stare. "You should have visited on Wednesday. Bernie was away all night, and I wasn't doing anything. I should have sent a little birdie to whistle for you."

He shakes his head, "Maureen . . ."

"If you miss these opportunities, Justin, they might never come again."

Justin says, "Maureen."

She looks away quickly, her sights careering. "Look at those clouds! Black as night. It's hard to believe there's such a thing as summer. They're saying on the radio that it will be a wet winter. Rain, rain, rain, as if cold old winter isn't bad enough. How is Aria, Justin?"

He says, "I never know who you're talking about when you say that name. We call Ariella *Plum*."

"Plum, Aria, Ariella: I haven't seen her all week. That's not like her. I gather something happened at her party — your mother said the guests went home suddenly, without explaining why. Is Plum all right? Is she well?"

Justin, for the first time, hesitates, glancing at the car and across it to the newspaper lying on the lawn, and then down the concrete driveway to her; and Maureen knows she has driven home a nail. In this moment she hears him sliding and sliding — wanting her wisdom, needing to shed the weight of the week, remembering that he trusts her and that she is the silver lining to his otherwise predictable world — and she stands saying nothing, letting him slide. He smears a raindrop from the roof of the Holden before meeting her eye. "No one's sure what happened. No one heard anything. They just turned around and left. Plum hasn't talked about it — not to us, anyway. She stays in her room most of the time."

"Something awful's happened, obviously. Those friends of hers — they're catty girls, the worst type. But have you actually *asked* what happened?"

Justin shakes his head, plucks a melaleuca spike from the car's roof; and Maureen realizes there's a hollowness at the core of his family, a fear of discovering what it is that turns inside the hearts of one another — and that they know about this failing, and are ashamed. "She'd tell us if she wanted to. Anyway, it's probably nothing. She's fourteen — everything is bad when you're fourteen. She'll forget about it."

Maureen smiles. She would go to him and slap him, cradle him, but it's impossible to cross the line. She says, "Who ever forgets anything about being fourteen?"

He doesn't answer immediately, flattening raindrops one by one. He's the kind of person whose trials are writ in water; but even he has waited by an unringing telephone, even he has futilely hoped, even he carries memories that continue to smart. A corner of his mouth pinches, and he looks at her. "What, then?"

"Well, *somebody* should talk to her. Otherwise she'll grow up feeling no one cared enough to bother."

"That's not how it is—"

"Of course it isn't. But that's how she'll remember it. You'll have to say something to her, Justin. This mustn't be ignored."

"But what do I say?"

"You'll think of the right thing."

"Maybe she doesn't *want* to talk—"

"She will. Underneath, she will. Be careful, though. No matter what you think, this is serious for Plum. Don't treat it like a joke." Maureen pauses to reflect, tapping the envelope in her hand. "It's a pity she doesn't have a sister. This is exactly the time when a girl needs a sister."

Justin looks up sharply. "Could *you* talk to her?"

Maureen's taken aback. "Me?"

"You'd be better at it than I would."

She can see the idea dawning on him like sunlight. "No," she says. "This is something *you* should do, Justin."

"But Plum likes you." The responsibility is a hot stone in his hands, he can't pass it on fast enough. "I think she'd *prefer* talking to you . . ."

Maureen sighs. On the footpath by her shoe a snail is inching painfully over the cement. "I suppose I could," she says eventually. "If the opportunity comes, I'll say something. Not for you, though — for her."

The change in Justin is instant; he smiles, once again boyish and easy, and Maureen is overcome, as she always is, with gratitude that he is hers. She could fly to the sky on the sheer brilliance of this truth. He will always need so much from her, and she will be infinite for him. In its bare bones, everything is simple, yet more incredible than life. In several swift footsteps she crosses the line, going to him because this new beginning must be acknowledged. He turns his face from her cupping hands so her lips meet his cheek rather than his lips, his wariness of discovery still deeply ingrained, but what matters for now is that he's returned. "You have to go," he mutters, and, "Don't worry," she says, "I'm going."

Cydar stands before the fish tanks, the light from the fluorescent lamps falling dustily around him. He knows that his face will be ghostingly lit, as he has seen so many faces lit; that green weeds will be wavering in the dark center of his eyes. He's never had a guest to the bungalow who wasn't riveted to this spot, the furied, the addled, the untrustworthy, the depressed, all of them lulled by the cruising of the fish. The aquariums cast over Cydar himself a cloak of etherealness: he knows that people think of tranquillity when they think of him, mistaking the placidity of the fish for a Franciscan simplicity in him. The only girl Cydar has ever really loved stood in this exact place one day and said, "These fish are glittering pieces of all the good things in you." And although Cydar didn't know everything about himself, he had known that she, like everyone else, was confusing him with somebody he'd long ago decided not to be; and that eventually she would discover this, and feel he'd somehow misled her.

Turning from the tanks, he checks his memory against a piece of paper that lies on the desk. On the sheet, in Cydar's compressed hand, is written a list of species. Alongside each species is a quantity and a price. Near the bottom of the page a final sum is underlined. One species has been crossed out and replaced with another, and there are places where his pen has hesitated, his gaze lifted to survey the tanks and their inhabitants: but Cydar is happy with his final decisions. The prices add up to a bruising amount, the list of species to sparsely-filled tanks — but the aquariums, like the world beyond the glass, have always been places of change.

Stepping back to the tanks, Cydar combs a net through the water with practiced sweeps, pinning two clown fish into a corner. They are released into the nearer of the two white-lidded buckets that stand at Cydar's feet, where they join hatchetfish, angelfish, oscars and mollies. Against the white plastic, the creatures are dazzling. Laying aside the net, Cydar counts the collected animals quickly, checking them against the list. He hesitates at the sight of the lionfish — then clamps down first one lid and then the other, buckling the catches tight.

Justin had said he would help carry the buckets, but he hasn't appeared; time shouldn't be wasted, however, so Cydar takes a bucket in each hand and walks stiff-legged through the jungle and down the driveway, to where the Holden is parked. He'd supposed his brother must be in the bathroom preening, and is somehow even more annoyed to find him sitting behind the steering wheel of the car. He pulls open the passenger door, glares sourly across the seats. "I thought you were going to help," he says.

Justin only looks at him briefly. "Get in."

The sound of the Holden's engine wakes Plum, who has slept in. She lies blinking into her pillow, groggily unsure what the morning means. What returns first is the sense of doom that has dogged her all week. Today will be another miserable journey inside her skin. Today she might feel the twang of the last lines that tie down her endurance, and she'll blow away. Then she remembers her resolution of the previous afternoon, her vow to stop fighting to make right what has gone wrong, her decision to live a small still life within the safe walls of this house. The outside world will be alien and perilous, but her home will be sanctuary.

And then, in a flash, she realizes it is Saturday—Saturday morning, no less, the best corner of the week. Plum feels a huge wearied thankfulness that makes her curl up into a ball. She's always wished to be one of those girls for whom school is as fun as a carnival, and the weekend a suffocating lull: but she has never been that way, and now she can stop trying to be. Abandoning all her ambitions might prove, Plum discovers, a relief.

It is only a week since the birthday party, but although there's still horror in recollecting the day, the day itself seems long gone, a distance stretching through blackness. During the great length of time between then and now Plum has attended to none of the things that seemed important in the days leading up to the party. She has not sluiced her ears in methylated spirit, nor conscientiously rotated the studs. The pain of infection having abated, she's almost forgotten about them. Now she reaches up, unsure what to expect. She twitches her lobes and probes the earrings, and the tiny diamonds feel ugly to her fingertips: but the studs turn easily in their holes, and do not hurt. That her ears have healed seems a victory — Samantha and Rachael and Dash could wound her, but they couldn't kill her. And the important thing is this: they won't get the chance to wound her again.

She hears her mother, downstairs, calling out something to her father — the newspaper is not in the kitchen but still out on the lawn. Plum decides that, if it doesn't rain, she'll take her roller skates outside. Since Sophie pulled them from her feet, Plum hasn't worn her birthday present, and the skates stand scuffless against a wall. While the Holden isn't in the driveway she can practice spinning and gliding, and staggering and collapsing. It won't be a graceful sight, but she doesn't need to worry. No one who sees her wobbling will use her ineptitude as a weapon, or spread a warped description that becomes the perfect truth.

The Holden reminds Plum of something else she has neglected: she hasn't been worrying about Justin's lost job. Probably he's driven off to leave the car parked in that out-of-the-way street and then spend the day wandering, constantly checking his watch. Cydar has told her not to interfere, and she hasn't; but she should have been worrying. Justin is the best thing in her world: it's important — it's a thousand times more important now — that he be all right. Among the few good things that survived the party, nothing must go wrong.

Maybe, if the rain stays away, she will ask to borrow David, and take him to the park. After all the torments of this arduous week, it would be nice to feel again the harmony her heart felt that day she took the child to the playground.

Plum stretches her legs, folds her hands on her belly. Her stomach doesn't feel quite as lumpen as usual — almost definitely, she's getting thinner. If she walks to the park, and then roller-skates, that will be exercise. But she could unpick her bicycle from the junk in the shed, and ride it around after dinner. She could stop eating raspberry tarts, and start eating vegetables. She could read Charles Dickens instead of *Dolly,* and watch documentaries instead of horror movies. She won't ever return to church, but she could aspire to be *pure* — not so much the girl on the cover of magazines, but the one that poets write poems for, the one whom wild animals don't fear. She could give herself a new name to match this self: Waterlily, or FlyFree. She could show Rachael and Dash and Samantha that she's above them, like a star.

Only yesterday afternoon Plum had resigned herself to being a clod of earth: this morning, she is a star. The electric clock-radio flips its numbers with a tiny click of metal against metal, reminding her that Saturday morning is already half-gone. Fa should have brought her breakfast by now, crooning, "Plummy, Plummy" to wake her. His dereliction stirs a growl of umbrage—but then, with Waterlily's wisdom, Plum sees the world from an aspect other than her own. She has kept her bedroom door tightly closed all week. She has borne an air of misery that the slightest word risked making worse. The unexpected result of her estrangement is this: no breakfast in bed. In leaving her uncatered-for, Fa is trying to help his daughter in his own, cack-handed way.

Plum rolls upright, puts her feet to the floor. "Time to get up," she tells the posters, the ornaments, the teddy bears. Time to get up before everything that's still good feels unwanted, like breakfast, and ends.

SHE CAN'T BELIEVE that the girl comes to her. She's spent all morning considering ways of dealing with this situation — mostly, the difficulty of maneuvering past the girl's closed window and drawn blind. When the doorbell rings Maureen rushes to answer it, thinking it might be Justin although she hasn't heard the return of the Holden from wherever he went with Cydar; yet she's habitually hopeful, and thus disappointed. The girl, however, is the next-best thing, a problem overcome; and through the girl, she melds to him. "Aria!" she cries. "I thought I'd lost you!"

Plum's cheeks, already pink, stain pinker. She'd hesitated at the foot of the Wilks' porch steps, assailed yet again. Plum knows that Maureen had come to the house on the night of the party, and that she had been turned away:

so Maureen must know how badly the party had failed. Seeing Plum, the first thing Maureen would think was, *All your friends left you.* She wouldn't think it out of unkindness, but because it was a fact. Mortification had loomed up from the ground, Plum had almost turned back . . . but avoiding this meeting forever would mean Rachael and Dash and Samantha had stolen Maureen just like they'd stolen Sophie. She had gritted her teeth, pressed her thumb into the bell. "I know!" she says now. "It's been ages!"

"Come in," says Maureen. "We're just finishing lunch."

Plum steps into the house, and the very perfect smell of it embraces her like nurse's arms — it occurs to her that the Wilks house, rather than her own, is the safest place in her world. Rachael has never knocked on its door, Dash does not know its telephone number, Plum's protected by Maureen's sophistication, which could wither Samantha like salt on a slug. She follows her friend into the kitchen, where David is perched on a stool, his hands attached as little anchors to the tiled counter. He's wearing denim overalls and a blue velour jumper, there's a plate of chewed crusts on a saucer before him. "Daddy?" he pipes, and Maureen says, "No, it's Aria."

"Hi, Davy." He's like seeing water after sand. "I was wondering if you'd come to the park with me? Play on the swings?"

The boy, deer-eyed, shakes his head. "I'm waiting for Daddy."

"Daddy's not here," says Maureen. "No daddy today, I've told you. Aria will push you on the swing. Coffee first, Aria?"

"Yes please," says Plum; David looks to his plate without comment. Plum takes the stool beside him and watches her neighbor moving around the kitchen, filling the kettle and placing it on the stove, opening a packet of Butternut Snaps. Maureen is fluid, like a ballerina, in everything she does. A tight-fitting turtleneck jumper shows how lean and long she is. It seems wrong that something so lovely is stuck here, in this ordinary place, a nugget of gold underground. Her husband is hardly home to admire her; in the whole time Plum has been taking notice, no visitors have come to her house. Yet unlike Fa, who has everything worth having yet is still somehow sad, Maureen seems content with what she has, and Plum is glad. If she were unhappy, Maureen might leave, and sitting at the counter Plum tastes, with shock, how frightening this would be. She needs Maureen as much as, maybe more than, she needs her mother and father. Her throat thickens: "It's nice to see you," she says, and must stop.

Maureen glances over a shoulder. "It's very nice to see you too, Aria."

Plum nods too many times, chews on her empty mouth. "I'm thinking about changing my name," she blurts. "To Waterlily. Or FlyFree."

Maureen laughs. "Awful! Like a feminine product. Don't

you dare. Have faith in yourself. Just be who you are."

"But being who I am isn't *good* . . . "

"Naming yourself Waterlily won't improve things, believe me."

"Waterlily is a frog's name," David opines.

Plum looks at him, and croaks like a frog, and the child chuckles, and his chuckling fills her with pleasure, so Plum croaks again. They giggle and croak while Maureen makes the coffee, and when she takes a seat opposite Plum with the mugs and a plate of biscuits between them she says, "Shush, you two! This is a house, not a pond. How has school been, Aria?"

She asks it as if she's ignorant of everything—Plum knows it's a chance to tell the truth or to duck it, and that the choice is hers. How childish she'll appear to Maureen, if she chooses wrong. She looks down into the circle of coffee, says, "Well" and "It's been . . ." and stops both times, her fingers dithering around the mug's handle. Her mouth tugs, her nose creases. When she lifts her head, Maureen must see the torment in her eyes: Maureen does see, and knows how surely she's won. "Not very good," Plum groans. "You can imagine."

Maureen moves a hand across the counter to rest two fingers on the girl's arm. "I can imagine, Aria," she says, "because I remember what it's like."

Plum's lip trembles. "It was all just—silly—"

"The worst things usually are. Silly, and murderous."

The girl nods slackly, without looking up. She goes to

speak but can scarcely breathe; then tries again, dredging up muddy words. "All my friends hate me."

"Hmm. Well, that happens sometimes. But you've never been absolutely sure of those girls, have you? You've never really liked them."

"But now they hate me!" Tears leap the brink and skid down Plum's cheeks — she hits them away forcefully. Her resolution to be star-like has crashed to earth already. She *wants* to have friends, even friends whom she doesn't like and who aren't always nice to her: having even *those* friends was better than being outcast and alone. She isn't strong or unconventional or stupid enough to survive this, she is going to die, she would *rather* be dead than live amongst the shards of this life. "They won't talk to me," she weeps. "Everyone's whispering about me. No one's going to be my friend."

Maureen doesn't say, *Don't be silly.* She says, "Whatever you did that caused this, you are still a good person, Aria. Don't let them make you think that you aren't."

An ursine noise comes from Plum — "hunuh!" — as if she's been knocked over. Tears flood down her cheeks, more tears than she's ever cried before. The prospect of recounting what happened at the party makes her feel bilious, makes the tears flow faster and brews another *hunuh* in her chest — yet she *must* tell, she's committed to telling, because otherwise the story will grow in her stomach like the hair-and-toothed tumor she once saw on TV. She needs someone to take the horror and hammer it into laughable particles which can be swept away. "Tell me what happened," Maureen prompts. "Maybe things aren't as ruined as you imagine."

"They are!" Plum's face crumples, and while David concentrates on the countertop and Maureen watches through eyes soft with concern, she wallows without caring that her face looks ugly and that her nose is blowing bubbles: she wants to cry, she has a *right* to cry, she's only fourteen and her life is ended, and she might have bawled all afternoon if Maureen had not said, "Aria, stop now. Crying fixes nothing, and you're scaring David." And her reluctance to frighten the little boy makes Plum sniff her desolation back into her head, makes her wipe her wet cheeks and soppy chin. "Sorry, Davy," she sighs, "it's all right," and the boy shoots a glance at her, deeply unsure. It isn't all right, but Plum has come too far to retreat. Her eyes roll around miserably until they fix on the tea towel folded over the oven rail. If she had other personalities, like Sybil in *Sybil,* she could make one of *them* tell the story; instead she must tell it herself, glaring at the tea towel with terrible eyes.

"I took some things from my friends. Not expensive things—little things. A yo-yo, and a penny, and a tiny glass lamb. A broken watch—that was Rachael's. An Abba badge that belonged to Dash. A charm bracelet from Sophie—it was her lamb, too. A jade necklace—not a fancy one. I was keeping them in a briefcase underneath my bed. At my party, they found the case."

"Ouch!" says Maureen. "I bet that took the fizz out of the lemonade."

The girl glances up shyly. "They were really angry."

"I'm sure they were! I'm sure they were delighted by the chance to be angry, too. I assume you had a reason for taking these things?"

Plum's gaze swings back to the towel. "It's hard to explain." Her mouth pinches, and tears spill again. "I thought that if I had these objects where I could see them and touch them and—sort of—*influence* them, I might make things *different*—I could make myself important, and they would *want* me to be their friend, they'd be *proud* that I'm their friend, and I wouldn't be so—kind of—*weak* all the time. I could be—sort of—*in charge*, sometimes. Or at least—not always on the bottom."

Maureen smiles around the mug's rim. "I think you've been watching too many voodoo movies in the middle of the night."

Plum swallows hard. "I guess. It was stupid."

"It wasn't stupid. It's not a crime to want respect. You shouldn't be ashamed of that. Perhaps you went about trying to get it the wrong way, that's all."

The unfairness of the world rises up in her throat. "I didn't even *want* the dumb necklace! I didn't want an ugly badge or a broken watch or any of that junk! I just— *needed*—"

"I know," soothes Maureen. "I understand. You needed

secret weapons. But you knew it wasn't going to work, didn't you? You know you can't change things just by touching a penny. All you've done is given your friends an excuse to make you more unhappy than they were already doing."

The girl's eyes leap to the woman's face, desperate for the wise words that will return light to her world. Maureen lets her thrash in darkness for a drawn-out moment before announcing, "You're better off without them, Aria. They're no loss to you. *You* are a loss to *them*. They'll understand this one day, but then it will be too late because we don't go back, we don't forgive. School will be a difficult place for you now—but it's always been difficult, hasn't it? You're strong, and you'll just have to get stronger. And you'll always have me, Aria. If it's any comfort, I promise I will always be your friend. No matter *what* you do."

The relief is so tremendous that a moan is pressed from Plum. "Thank you," she sighs. Then laughs wheezily: "I'm always saying *thank you* to you."

"You needn't. I've told you before: I'm glad we're friends."

"You don't think I'm awful?"

"For stealing from your friends?" Maureen takes a Butternut Snap from the plate and breaks it into parts. "Do *you* think you're awful?"

"Only a little bit. Not much."

"I agree. I think you're naughty, but I don't think you're awful."

Naughty makes Plum chuckle. She takes a biscuit, sits

straighter, pulls a funny face at the boy. Her eyes are drying, her heart is buoyed: to Maureen she confesses, "I was scared to tell you. I thought you'd hate me."

"I'm honored you told me. It shows you trust me."

"I do trust you!" A speck of Butternut Snap jumps to the counter. "I'd rather have you as my *only* friend than have *ten* of those others!"

"Thank you," says Maureen. "And I trust you. Shall I tell you my secret, in exchange for yours?"

"Ooh!" Plum has not expected this, and hunkers forward. "Yes! Tell me!"

"All right." Maureen smiles. "Aria: your brother Justin and I are involved. We have a relationship — do you understand? We love one another. We have done for a long time."

She tells it plainly, so the girl won't be confused, yet Plum stares as if she's never possessed a brother Justin, never encountered this word *love*. Bafflement crosses from one eyebrow to the other: she asks, "Are you going to get — married?"

"I think so. Probably."

"But what about your husband?"

Maureen grimaces. "These things happen, Aria."

Plum feels as if she's opened her bedroom window to discover not the familiar view of roofs and mountains, but a world weirder than the deepest sea. The tea towel, the kettle, the shining sink are all utterly bizarre. The blackbird calling outside is a sound she's never heard. Even Maureen is suddenly a stranger, a woman about whom Plum knows nothing. There are probably grand things that should be said, but she doesn't know what they are. "What about him?" she asks, of the child at her elbow.

Maureen frowns. "David will be fine."

The jabbering discord of Plum's confusion clears for an instant: "I'll be his auntie," she realizes. "I'll be your auntie," she tells the boy. "You'll be my nephew, Davy! And your mummy — she'll be my sister-in-law! Won't that be good? You can live here, and I'll live next door, and we can see each other every day!"

The boy smiles uneasily, looks across at his mother. "I'm not sure about that, Aria," says Maureen. "It might be Bernie who stays in this house."

"What?" Plum gapes. "What? No! I want you to stay here! Where would you go?"

"Possibly to Berlin," Maureen replies. "Justin and I have discussed it."

It takes Plum a moment to locate the city on the map, but when she does she is appalled. "But — that's so far away! How will you and Justin be together, if you go to Berlin?"

Maureen laughs fondly. "Aria, you're so quaint. Justin will be coming to Berlin too. We'll be going together. We're going to rent an apartment. We've discussed it, I told you."

The girl stares while the revelation runs through her like spillage down a drain. "Justin can't go to Berlin," she says.

"No? Why can't he?"

"Because—" Plum fumbles. "Because he's my brother!"

"Aria," says Maureen. "You can't keep him forever."

Plum peers, dumbfounded, into this new upturned world. Words lunge out of her: "When? When are you going?"

"As soon as we're able. Very soon, I hope."

Plum's mouth opens and shuts. Everything is helter-skelter. Her eyes feel pulled unnaturally wide, her ears hear a hollow ring. Her whole body hurts like it's been thrown into a wall. This is the worst thing that's ever happened to her. "I don't want Justin to go away," she says, in a voice like a gravel road. "I don't want *you* to go away, either. What about me?"

"Oh Aria, you'll be fine. I know you—I know how strong you are. You think you're not, but you *are*. And you can visit during school holidays—wouldn't you like that?"

"No," says Plum. "I'd like it better if you stayed here."

"I know." Maureen winces. "But it's all planned now. Maybe, when you're old enough, you could spend a few months with us, or even a year? I'd love that—wouldn't you?"

The prospect sparks no enthusiasm in Plum: she sits like a toy that's been too tightly wound, packed with energy yet paralyzed, her gaze flat and unseeing. "I didn't know about any of this."

"No, but you almost did! Do you remember thinking that Justin had a secret? Well, *I'm* his secret. Everything I've just told you is our secret. No one knows about any of this yet — you're the first. Isn't that exciting?"

Plum is being hit by waves of shock that are knocking her down and tumbling her over, making it difficult to think; in the distance is rising the greatest wave, which will arrive in wrath and thunder. This tidal wave is sucking the oxygen from the room, leaving her, for the moment, muted and suppressed. "I was going to take David to the park," she says.

"Yes, you were!" Maureen stands quickly, as if she too senses the coming torrent. "David, go with Aria. It's a nice afternoon for the park."

Plum waits outside on the porch while the child's shoes are found. The tidal wave is coming and she doesn't try to escape it, but waits with a simmering calm. She squints up at the sky, which has lost its cloudiness and cleared to pale blue. "Be a good boy for Aria," Maureen tells her son; and the great wave blocks the light of the sun when Plum thinks, *I hate that name, Aria.*

Justin stays out of the way while Cydar makes the deal, strolling alone down the dim corridors as he does every time his brother persuades him to come out to this warehouse which is as temperate as an island, surreal as LSD. Hundreds of fish tanks line the aisles along which Justin walks, hands in pockets, stopping occasionally to admire an octopus or a turtle or, on one memorable occasion, a medium-sized crocodile. "Buy the crocodile," Justin had urged, but Cydar had said, "No," without even trying to pretend he might. This place is all business, for Cydar. If Justin listened to the conversation being conducted between his brother and the undefinably distasteful man who owns the warehouse, he would hear numbers slamming their heads together like rams, bargains driven home like fists. The first time he'd heard such cool gray language from his brother, Justin had been startled. He'd assumed the fish were pets to Cydar. "Won't you miss them?" he'd asked that day, trailing his brother out to the car; Cydar was riffling through a wad of notes and didn't look up to answer, "Nothing's irreplaceable."

In every visit since, Justin has walked the aisles with their concrete floors and their walls made of glass, saying little and thinking less, feeling the weight of wet air in his lungs, slowing but not stopping when some peculiar creature catches his eye. The tanks are glowingly lit, stacked high upon one another like ingots. If he passes the gangly kid who cleans the tanks, Justin will say, "How you doing," and the kid in his damp T-shirt will answer, "G'day." Other than this, Justin bites back his opinion, for it's that kind of place, like a cemetery. The churning of filters is like the reciting of prayers. He hears but makes no comment on what's being said in the corner near the till; he waits for Cydar to find him among the heavenly aisles, then asks, as if it isn't obvious, "Ready?" Sometimes, on the way to the door, he'll point out an interesting specimen.

Cydar assesses the beast in a glance, unfailingly keeps walking.

Today Justin's thoughts won't be stilled, as they usually are when at the fish dealer's. He casts his mind off like a boat, only to have it nudgingly return. He should not have talked to Maureen in the front garden this morning. She's in his life the way the warehouse air is in his chest, invasive, too heavy. He should have turned his back on her. From now on he will; he's impatient to. But he should have done so this morning.

"Let's go." Cydar's suddenness makes Justin jump. In this aquatic world, he is a cat. The twin white buckets are swinging empty at his knees, his pockets will be plugged with cash he'll use not in a free and joyful way, but coldly, reasonedly. Justin waves a hand down a fog-lit aisle: "Come and see. There's this fish called a sargrassy or something—"

"Sargassum," says Cydar. "No. We've got things to do."

Justin sighs, and heads for the door; but he could do with a touch of Cydar's hard-bittenness. It would make life cleaner, less tatty. And Cydar, thinks Justin, has some ruthlessness to spare.

Plum walks David to the milk bar because she needs something sugary in her mouth: two slabs of coconut ice are dropped in a paper bag, along with three Sherbet Bombs that use up the last of her change. They go then to the playground in the park, where Plum and the boy sit side-by-side on the bench in the shade of the plane tree. The grass looks fresh and glossy, and at the edge of the tanbark bees chug from daisy to daisy. "Be careful of the stings," Plum warns the child. "Here," she says, pushing into his hand a chunk of coconut ice. David feeds it without hesitation into a corner of his mouth. "Do you like it?" Plum asks—he nods and answers, "Hmm-hmm." His small mild presence is keeping the cataclysmic wave at bay, but the longer it waits, the stronger it grows. The children both eat methodically, contemplating the empty playground. "Swing?" Plum suggests, when David's finished the confection and is shaking coconut from his fingers in a finicky, disgusted way. They cross the tanbark to where the swings dangle from their chains, and he fits himself with neatness onto the wooden seat.

"Berlin!" She blows the words past her teeth with the first heave against the swing. David arcs forward, legs stiff as tongs. "Do you know where that is, Davy? Miles away. Far across the seas. . . . That sounds like a fairy-tale place, doesn't it? *Far across the seas.*"

The boy is whisked high by the strength in Plum's arms and hangs his head as the swing swoops skyward, laughing enchantedly. Plum steps away as she reaches for the swing, steps forward again with each push, settling into a rhythm that keeps the child soaring at a steady height and pace. Out in the dark distance, the wave has begun to move—David, so unobtrusive, can't fend it off forever. The black water is yawning like a monster's maw. "I think she's mean, your mother," says Plum. "She's mean, mean, mean. I thought she was my friend, but all this time she's been scheming to go away and leave me. *And* to take my brother. And she wants me to be happy about it! *You can visit during school holidays:* yeah, sure, I bet that won't happen. Who will be my friend now, Davy? *Nobody.* I won't even be able to push you on the swings, because she'll take *you* away from me too."

The boy replies with a gargle of laughter — Plum curls her lip, reaches up, shoves the swing as she'd like to shove the world. "Your mum is always saying, *You can tell me anything, Aria. You can trust me, I'm your friend.* But she keeps secrets — secrets about stealing all my best things from me. That's not what a friend does, is it, David? That's not being trustworthy. That's sly, isn't it? She said she was my friend, when she was really my enemy. She's a liar, your mother. A dirty *liar.*"

The edge of the swing slams into her palms, and she puts her weight into sending it away. The boy, who has no weight, flies like a feather in a hurricane, his hands clammed to the chains. "I thought she liked me." The tidal wave is boiling and cluttered. "But she's as bad as Sophie. Deserting me. She's as bad as Caroline, running away. She reckons I can look after myself, but that's *easy* for her to say. She's not the one being *left.* She'll have everything *she* wants. And she'll — she'll — she'll have Justin."

Plum hasn't yet given thought to the romantic aspects of the situation: now, with the afternoon sun on her head and the air steamy with vaporizing rain and the swing returning reliably and the tidal wave looming just off the shore, she cautiously considers the matter. *Justin and I love one another.* The words have a cartoon-like horror. Justin and Maureen kissing, twining their limbs, dreaming of each other, taking off their clothes: Plum's mouth twists at the idea, she pushes the image away. Into its place springs something more sinister, a realization so scorching that it makes Plum gasp. It is *Justin* whom Maureen has cared about all this time. Justin was loved, and Plum was . . . used. The invitations to the garden, the soft drink and cupcakes, the sisterly concern, the understanding smiles, the earrings, the blue dress: "It was for Justin," she tells the boy, who doesn't reply, his legs whipping loosely at the knees. "Not for me—for *Justin.* She was using me to send messages to Justin."

And Plum gulps with the sorrow of it, remembering the bearish affection she'd felt for the woman, how deeply she'd laid her trust in her. She feels blood pooling in her cheeks, water leaking from the corners of her eyes. The swing flies upward, trailing giggles like ribbon: "Higher!" yips the boy. Plum grits her teeth, pushes harder. The tidal wave is overhanging her head now, a massive black crest, a nightmare. "Your mother's a bitch," Plum hisses. "Can you say that, Davy? *Bitch.*" And the water is coming down on her now, crashing green water which carries in its depths all the agonies of fourteen and which sweeps her up easily, throws her head over heels. In her whole life, the only thing that shines is Justin, the only thing Plum wants to keep is Justin, the one thing she'd lie down and *die for* is Justin; without Justin, there's no rescue, no escape, no point. Everything else she can survive—she can survive without friends, without Maureen, with living a little life, she can *thrive*—but not this, not Justin, not her best and favorite thing, her Justin . . . Plum thinks, then, something unspeakable: *she would prefer it if he died.* Rather than lose him to Maureen, Justin could die. Such a loss would have tragic beauty. This loss is too ugly to bear. That loss would be everyone's. This loss is only hers.

"I hate." Plum tumbles over and over, malevolent and afraid. "He is not hers, I hate."

"I am flying," says David.

"He can't be hers. I hate her. I wish she'd die. I wish she wasn't born." Thrown about in the water, she's battered and dizzied; words pour out with each breath and race like bubbles to the surface. "It's crazy, isn't it? It's crazy. Your mother is crazy, David. Justin doesn't *love* her—how *could* he? He never talks about her. They never go out together. He never visits her house, she never visits ours. And she's *married,* don't forget. She's already *got* a husband. So how could he like her? He *couldn't.* It's just stupid. It's Maureen being stupid. Probably she was drunk. I'm not going to be friends with her now, even if she *was* drunk. She's too much of a schemer. She's an awful person—"

Plum surfaces, snatching at air—she sees the swing flying over her head, sunlight glinting across the white sky.

Moving along swiftly in the grip of the wave, she thinks over what she's just said. Most of it is true. The idea of Berlin and a love affair makes no sense at all. It couldn't happen, and it won't.

But Maureen is never stupid, not in any of the ways the word can mean. And there's something more, something elusive that the tidal wave hauls from Plum's grip every time her fingertips brush against it. Something that runs off when her memory calls it, but is also being deliberately chased away. Dread freezes in her spine at the thought of what she'll know once this slick thing stops running and reveals itself. "That's enough swinging," she abruptly tells David. "You'll sick up your coconut ice."

The boy climbs awkwardly from the stopped swing. His cheeks are colored like apples, polished by the cold wind. He smooths his clothes and smiles up at her. Noticing the diamonds in her ears, he points and smiles again. "Twinkle."

"Yeah." The idea of stealing him crosses her mind — lifting him up and hurrying off in a new direction, thieving him as Maureen wants to thieve Justin, never returning to that stinky old house or to that evil school, but forging for both of them fresh lives. They could run away to the countryside, where nobody would recognize them. People would think she was his mother, and David would forget he'd ever had a proper one. It is what Maureen and Justin deserve. Except, of course, that it isn't *true*, Justin doesn't deserve anything because logically *none of this can be true* — it's a huge relief to remember the impossibility of it being true. "Hold my hand," she tells the child.

"Can we see Justin's car?"

Plum's head whips around, she stares down at the boy. The elusive thing that is running skids to a smoky halt. She sees Justin's car parked in the shade of a paperbark in an out-of-the-way street, and no reason that she could guess for its being there.

The tidal wave has left her beached, breathless and dripping. The sun seems too bright for this wintry day, the air sharp like the edges of paper. "Davy," she says, "does my brother Justin ever come to visit you at your house?"

The boy squints. *Don't answer,* Plum wants to say. "One day," he sighs. "Sometimes." And Plum, heartbroken, looks away, grappling with the small hand. Justin, and Maureen. And Cydar — even Cydar, in whom she's always had faith. All of them have lied, letting her think that she can be safe.

"Liars," she whispers. "Lie, lie, lie." David's fingers knot inside hers. Justin's car, Plum recollects, had been parked beneath the paperbark on the afternoon she babysat the boy because Maureen *needed the afternoon.* "You and me." She rubs her eyes and peers down at him, and can't bear to look at anything except the face of the child. "They used us, Davy. We're just nothing to them. They don't care about either of us. You and me, we should go away."

℘ JUSTIN STEPS OUT OF THE BUNGALOW as Plum and the boy are coming through the garden, both children keeping to the track that weaves through the miscellany of thistle and destitute flower-beds. She's marching so determinedly that the boy must jog, captured by her grip on his wrist. Her face is set in anger, and the first thing Justin thinks is that it's the child who is the subject of her rage; and although it's dangerous to speak to David and invite the disasters of what the boy might say, a volt of protectiveness spears Justin: "Don't drag him, Plum," he says. "He's only got short legs."

Plum stops, a wasteland of weeds and geranium scrawling between herself and her brother. She pulls the child to her hip. "What do you care?" she says loudly. "You don't care about him. You don't care about anyone."

In all his life Justin has never been the subject of her rancor. Mums and Fa, and sometimes Cydar, and her teachers and sundry others who cross her path: but never him. He shades his eyes, as if he's not seeing her properly. "What?"

"Maureen told me about you and her, and how the two of you are going away."

The bald, somehow untidy statement leaves Justin and even Plum herself vaguely staggered. "What?" Justin says again.

"Don't act stupid!" Plum shrieks, and David flinches but can't hide, and Justin feels her loudness like a punch against the jaw. "You know what I'm talking about! Were you ever going to tell me? Were you ever going to tell Mums and Fa? Or were you just going to sneak away like a — a *rat*?"

The bungalow door wheezes and Cydar steps out, a cigarette sloping between his fingers, his black-snake eyes aware of everything. "You're scaring him," he warns, meaning the boy, and Plum understands: but it is Justin who spins toward him, grateful. "What are you screaming about, Plum?"

Plum kicks a skin of soil from the path. "You shut up, Cydar! Don't pretend to be dumb. You know what's going on. Well, I know it too now. Maureen told me the big stupid secret. She and Justin are *in love,* and now they're *running away*."

Justin laughs like he's been shockingly slapped. Cydar takes a long draw from his cigarette, sliding his eyes to his brother. "Is that true?"

"No!" Justin cries. "Of course not!"

"Well why would she say it, if it wasn't true?"

Justin wheels to his sister. "I have no idea!"

"Maybe because she's crazy?"

Justin grabs it like a drowner. "She must be!"

Plum smiles gruesomely, flexing her fingers around David's wrist. "Yeah, that's what I reckoned. That would be silly. You wouldn't be in love with her. But then I asked David, and he said you visit their house sometimes."

"David's a little kid, Plum! He doesn't know what he's talking about! He'll say anything you want him to say!"

"Yeah," Plum agrees stonily. "I thought that too. You can't trust what a kid says. But then I remembered your car."

Justin, standing under the open sky, holds up his hands defenselessly. Unpracticed at having to protect himself, nothing comes to his aid. The brothers and their sister stare at each other in silence while a brown myna ticks its way across the bungalow roof and a cabbage moth dips from flower to flower. Justin looks to Cydar, and when he sees the darkness in his brother's face he laughs in astonishment. "Cydar! You're joking!"

Because Cydar, who has always distrusted the world, is suddenly seeing there's no reason why Justin shouldn't prove himself untrustworthy as well. Deceit is such an ordinary thing, and Justin is an ordinary man. He gives his brother the thinnest of glances, taps ash into the ash-ridden dirt. "What did Maureen say, Plum? Don't scream it, just say it."

Plum raises her chin. "She told me that she and Justin love each other—that they've loved each other for a long time. That they're probably going to get married, and that they're going to live in Berlin."

Justin gives an incredulous bark. Cydar's gaze crosses the weeds to his brother. "That sounds very happily-ever-after."

Justin goes to reply but only gapes, empty hands hanging. A strange calm moves through him, and when he speaks, the panic has been smoothed from his voice. "Cydar, it's not true. Believe me. I don't know anything about this. There's just me—you know me." And although Cydar ponders him for another instant, Justin sees him remembering that they do know each other—that this family which has never fitted quite snugly together is none-theless bonded and reliable. Relieved, he turns back to his sister and says, "I don't know why Maureen told you those things, Plum. But why do you believe her? Just because she said it, that makes it true?"

Uncertainty flickers inside the girl, she almost takes all her accusing words back; but the Holden is evidence made of steel, and she says, "I've seen your car parked near the playground on days when you were supposed to be at work. What was it doing there?"

Justin hesitates; a smile scratches his face. "I work in a bottle shop," he replies. "I deliver flagons to old ladies who can't carry them home on the bus. I deliver cartons of beer to men who get the shakes if they leave the house. Sometimes I stay and talk to them, because, besides something to drink, what they want is someone to talk to while they're drinking. That's probably what I was doing when you saw the car: talking about grandchildren and eating fruitcake. That's what I am, Plum—a delivery guy. Not someone who runs off to Berlin."

Cydar looks away, blows smoke from his nose. Plum stands swaying slightly, depleted by confusion. Beyond the geraniums is *Justin,* the brother of whom she is so proud. The one who races her up the stairs, eats the unwanted food from her plate, teases her about rock stars, lets her carry off his spare change. "Why would I like Maureen?" he is asking. "Why would I want to *marry* her, let alone go away with her? She's already got one husband who can't stand being in the house with her. She's *old,* too—she's an old married housewife with a kid. Why would I like that, Plum? What's in it for me?"

This morning such words would have been sacrilege; now she stares longingly over the weeds at him, wanting and wanting to believe. Wanting to keep him for as long as she needs him; wanting an end to the demolition of the cornerstones of her life. Wanting the humiliation of having to apologize. She wipes a wrist across her dry lips. "So she made it up?"

"She must have. Because I swear it isn't true."

And, indeed, he seems appalled. He looks like he's been confronted by a pack of hostile dogs. Plum wants to believe him, and discovers that she does: yet threads of perplexity catch and pull. She asks, "But why would Maureen say it, if it isn't true? She already has everything. Why would she pretend she has you?"

"I don't know. Maybe she's not — well. She's a bit — funny, don't you think?"

Plum muses. "At night she walks outside in her dressing gown. That's strange."

"She gave you diamonds. That was strange too."

"She stares at our house like an exorcised ghost," contributes Cydar from the door — the siblings think of the films they've watched together, and know exactly what is meant. "She's always hugging me and touching me and saying she understands me." Plum has warmed to the task. "She wants to be a teenager, even though she's old."

"She's comical," says Justin.

"Not comical," corrects Cydar. "She tries too hard, that's all."

"So why would I like her?" Justin looks back to his sister. "Maureen's silly. She's sad."

Plum nods, shifting her grip on David's wrist. Now that the word has been pinned to her, Plum sees that Maureen *is* sad. It's sad that she would sabotage her good-enough life by making up stories. It's sad she could imagine that somebody like Justin would love her. If she's a bit crazy, that too is sad.

But Plum doesn't feel sad: she feels a pinpoint anger that has a precise name. *Insult.* She has trusted Maureen, been honest with her, sought solace in their friendship, credited Maureen with fine thoughts and sympathy—and in return Maureen has given a brutal kick to Plum's already somersaulting world. In doing so, Maureen is not merely sad: she's as bad as, or worse than, Plum's school friends. Justin says, "I don't think you should be friends with Maureen, Plum," and Plum, from the heights of white-lipped dudgeon, replies, "No. I couldn't be."

"I'll take David home," says Cydar, stepping away from the bungalow door.

"No, I'll do it." Plum pushes the boy behind her legs. "I want to. I want to see her one last time. After that, we won't be friends."

Justin and Cydar watch their sister walk away, leading the lamb-like child by the hand. The overgrown shrubs bob and waver in their wake. When she's rounded the house and disappeared, Justin turns to his brother. Cydar thinks he looks exhausted, and older than he had been. "Thanks," says Justin, with the good grace to be ashamed; and Cydar, who is not the type to dissect what's done, only drops his cigarette butt into the dirt and crushes it with a toe.

Plum leads David to the front door, and presses the bell. She is not nervous, although she supposes she should be. She is, rather, like a saint going to the pyre, brave because she's sure that she has right on her side. After a decorous pause, Maureen opens the door. "Aria! David!" As if she's never expected to see them again. "Come inside! Did you have a lovely time?"

"We played on the swings." Plum will keep to the facts. "You swung really high, didn't you, David? And we ate coconut ice. Then we went to my house, and talked to Justin and Cydar. There was a moth in the garden, wasn't there, David? A big white fluttery one."

The boy is wandering away down the hall, listing toward the wall. "Come inside, Aria," says Maureen. "I'll get you a glass of cordial." So Plum follows her neighbor through the house to the kitchen, where David has tucked himself beneath the overhang of the counter. She can see that Maureen is jumping with curiosity, and it makes Plum want to snigger. Maureen is always trying to be mysterious, like a hieroglyphic: suddenly she's as plain as a blackboard. Stopped in the doorway, Plum throws her a scrap: "I told Justin what you said — that you and him love each other."

"Oh yes?" The words snap on the air. She's filling a beaker with water, looking across the kitchen at Plum, her back very rigid, her eyes wide. She would scramble out of her skin if she could.

So Plum is deliberate. "I thought you wouldn't mind if I told him that I knew. You said it was a secret, but it couldn't be a secret from *him*."

Water rises to the beaker's rim; quickly Maureen turns off the tap.

"Cydar was there," Plum adds conscientiously, "so he heard what Justin and I were saying. I hope that's all right? I couldn't tell him to go away."

"I did tell you it was a secret, Aria. You should have respected that. Still, everyone has to know eventually."

Plum shrugs. "Yeah, I guess. I didn't tell Mums or Fa, though."

"What did Justin say?"

"I'm not going to tell them, so you don't need to worry."

Maureen crosses the kitchen with a green drink for her son. She has forgotten to make one for the visitor. "What did Justin say, Aria?"

Plum tips her head against the wall, lets her gaze rove to the ceiling. There's a cobweb in the corner that has somehow escaped notice. "He was a bit surprised."

Maureen wraps the boy's hand around the beaker. "Drink it. What do you mean?"

"Well, he said he doesn't love you, for a start. He said that you give him the creeps, looking at our house all the time."

For all her nonchalance, Plum's heart is racing. The kitchen wall is painful against her temple. She knows how barbarous she is being, and what Mums would say to this. She knows, too, that she's walking an edge—that there's something unpredictable in this situation. But like the saint going to the pyre, she has a final and glorious chance to castigate a foe: and every word is a small revenge for what's happened and will happen to her.

Maureen has straightened, and is staring at her. "I can't help looking at your house. It's outside my window. You often look into my garden from your bedroom window, don't you?"

"Yeah, but that isn't what he meant. He laughed, when I told him he was marrying you. He said you've already got a husband, even if he's never in the same place as you. Justin said you're a housewife with a husband and a baby, and what would he want with that? I think he'd prefer someone *newer*, you know? Somebody more like him. You'd be kind of *secondhand*. Oh, and that's another thing: he said you're too old. You're not *really* old, but you're too old for someone like him. I mean, you're *much* older than him, aren't you? So it would be stupid. You wouldn't understand each other. You'd have nothing to talk about. Because Justin doesn't care about the kind of things *you* do. He doesn't care about furniture and magazines and everything. He'd just think it was dumb, caring about stuff like that."

Maureen is as still and failingly beautiful as a stuffed cheetah in a museum. She stares at Plum with glassy eyes, the boy huddled at her feet. "You're being unkind, Aria."

"I'm just telling you what he said!" Plum's pained. "You said you wanted to know. Justin said you must have been *joking,* what you said about you and him. He didn't mean it nastily, but he said, *What's to love about her?*"

Maureen's gaze shifts down to her son, who hides his face behind the beaker. She doesn't reply for several moments, in which Plum hardly breathes. "I don't believe you," she says.

Plum shrugs indifferently. "Oh, yeah," she adds: "He said you were funny. *Comical,* he said."

The woman slightly tilts, then rights herself. Scarlet blood is infusing her throat. Plum knows she will never stand in this kitchen again, and accepts this fallout willingly; but she takes a final look at David. He has been a pure thing in these last soiled weeks, and she will miss him. She pities him having to grow up in this house with this mother, but she supposes he will be all right. Most people appear to be all right, and whatever becomes of him, it won't make a difference to Plum's life. She has Justin; she can change schools and make new friends; the worst that can happen has happened, and things will get better from here. Soon, she'll probably be very happy. The likelihood of which prompts her to advise, "Don't worry, Maureen. You have a nice house and a nice family. That's enough, isn't it? Why should you want more? Why do you want my brother, too?"

"I would like you to leave now," says Maureen.

Plum doesn't argue, but pushes away from the wall and walks down the hall, the hair standing up on her arms because Maureen is following her, which at first is worrying but then suggests that she's not as angry as Plum has assumed her to be. At the front door the girl turns, ready to be on polite terms if that's what her neighbor wants. They will never be friends again, what Maureen did was too peculiar and cruel: but Plum has sufficient pity to spare for someone she once admired. The girl and the woman face each other, Plum on the concrete porch and Maureen on the hard-wearing mat, and their history of mutual loneliness skips through the moment and might once more have linked them, but Maureen says clearly, "Maybe your friends are right to hate you."

EVENING COMES IN WITH SUDDENNESS. It is afternoon, and then it is dusk, and the sensation is of drifting under a spell or of losing time intergalactically, to the gentle ministrations of almond-eyed extraterrestrials. The clouds that have lingered on the outskirts of the sky move in, gritty and dented. Sparrows speed to their roost in the conifers as shadows glide over the roofs. Cardigans are shaken from dresser drawers. Doors are closed against the dark. Then dusk is gone, and it's night again.

Plum slips her arms into the sleeves of a windcheater that has sat, fatly folded, in her cupboard for months. The garment had fit last winter; now her wrists show beyond the cuffs. She runs her palms down her chest, feels the bumps of her breasts and the ridge where her ribs meet her soft belly. The fleece feels odd against her sun-roughened skin; and sheathed in the windcheater it is easy to believe she won't see her body again until autumn and winter and blustery spring have passed. Underneath the shroud of her clothing, she will change. When she next sheds her covering, Plum will be something different.

Rain starts to fall, striking her window. Her blind is closed so she can't see the rain, but hears its *tat tat,* a raven's beak on the pane. In minutes the rain becomes heavier, chasing the raven away.

In the rubbish bin down the side of the house, where puddles of water collect when it rains and nibble at the house's red stumps, is stuffed Plum's cornflower-blue party dress. Part of her had argued against throwing the garment away, because she doesn't own another really stylish dress. It was childish, this part had protested, to take out her hurt on a piece of clothing.

But keeping the dress was impossible. It was mortally marred. Plum had accepted the inevitable, and had in fact felt some relief as she knotted the dress and dumped it amid the garbage bags. Her eyes were dry as mirages, although she'd wept in the hours since arriving home from Maureen's. All the cockiness that had supported her in her neighbor's kitchen had abandoned her, leaving her mauled and ill. Plum had expected Maureen to react as a snail does when tapped on the eye, with immediate and humble retreat: instead she'd done what Samantha would, or Dash. *Maybe your friends are right to hate you.* There's something wrong about a grown-up who could be so nasty to a young girl. Plum had felt as if all her bones had been disengaged from one another. She'd put her face into her pillow and wept.

But then something in herself had stepped away, and unexpectedly Plum found she detested the girl writhing and sniveling on the bed. "Stop crying," she told herself, and she had stopped. "Don't cry again," she'd said. "I'm sick of it."

It was a cold dead voice that addressed her, the sort of voice that tolerated no excuses, and Plum was too startled to offer it any. She'd turned over and sat up, looking around through waterlogged eyes. "What shall I do?" she'd asked herself, and it occurred to her that she could telephone Sophie, and try to explain. Say she was sorry, which, Plum discovered with surprise, she was.

She had wiped her eyes and turned them toward the window that had been, in these past weeks, the portal to a world that was more potent than she'd imagined. Nothing could be salvaged of the incandescent friendship she'd had with Maureen; the dress, like so many lunches, would have to go in the bin. When she thought of Maureen, the feeling Plum felt most was remoteness. But she would miss David. Maybe, in time, she'd find a way to talk to him without Maureen knowing. Maybe Plum could help him in small ways, the way his mother had almost helped her.

She'd climbed from the bed, taken the dress from its hanger, and gone outside to the bin. Later, at the dinner table, she'd been more talkative than she had been for days. Mums and Fa had beamed like sunflowers, delighted to have her back. Her parents, Plum knows, want her to be happy. They would be disappointed about the briefcase and her behavior toward Maureen; but if they knew the neediness behind her crimes, they would forgive her. They might even be proud of her. After such an unappetizing week, Plum had eaten her dinner with gusto. It had been a day like tumbling into terrifying water: it's amazing to think this is still the same day that had begun with the sound of the Holden driving away. She's been in black water, she's almost been drowned; but she's climbed up the bank, stunned and gasping, and she's safe now. Alive, and, though in pieces, still in one piece.

The late-late movie is *Duel,* which Plum has read about in her film encyclopedia but never actually seen. It occurs to her that she should keep a diary, a log book of the movies she's seen, the date she saw them, and perhaps a few lines of personal opinion. A leather-bound book that would become a bible of sorts, something to peruse on a rainy evening like this, something to preserve her past and guide her future. The rain is coming down heavily now, pummeling the window, making the world private. Downstairs, Fa will be collecting buckets to catch the leaky roof. Plum bends closer to her mirror and, concentrating on her reflection, unclips the diamond earrings and slips them from her ears. The tiny things glimmer in her palm. Diamonds aren't for throwing into rubbish bins, the way dresses are. But she will let the hard-won piercings close over, because a girl with pierced ears is not really who she is. She puts the earrings in their velvet case and pushes the box to the depths of her dresser drawer.

The mirror shows that Plum's hair is longer than she's realized, and of a bluer shade of black. Her eyes are curved across the top, giving them a friendly look. Her cheeks are spotted, but that's her age; she has no eternal moles. Her nose and mouth are still blurred by childhood, but promise to be acceptable. She pushes up the windcheater, frowns critically at her breasts. They look like two *crèmes brûlées* turned out from dessert bowls. She wonders if it's time to ask Mums to buy a bra. She's lived in dread of making this request, but suddenly she feels ready.

The knock on her door makes her spring back from the mirror, patting down her windcheater as if it were on fire. Flustered, she opens the door to see Cydar, the least expected of visitors, slouched against the balustrade. In his arms is a big brown box around which he's wrapped a pink ribbon but no paper, despite the fact that the box's contents are emblazoned in black letters on its side. "Can I come in?" he asks, and because her hands are clapped to her mouth, he steps in uninvited. He puts the box on her bed, and as she undoes the silky ribbon and lifts the television from its scaffolding Styrofoam, all she can say is, "Oh! Oh!" Cydar stands back among the posters while she pulls at plastic bags and electric coil, saying nothing until she looks at him with sparkling eyes and laughs, "Cydar, you remembered!"

"Happy birthday," he says.

"Cydar!" she shrieks; and is overcome by a physical frenzy, leaping up and down on the bed, thrashing her arms in the air. It is exactly the set she has hankered for — the three stubby legs are there, and the alien's antenna, and the helmet-like sphere of shiny chrome within which the black-and-white screen sits — and been forced to forget, because of the crushing cost. Suddenly suspicious, she rolls upright. "Where did you get so much money?"

"I sold the fish."

Plum's smile fades: "Not — all of them?"

"Most of them."

"The golden tang?"

"Yeah, the tang."

"The neon goby?"

"Most of them, Plum."

Plum sees row after row of phantasmal tanks reaching to the ceiling, each one white and still as a headstone. She sees Cydar lying in the dark, his searching eyes seeing nothing. Anguish rears in her: "But you loved your fish."

Her brother shrugs. He would never say there are other things to love. "It doesn't matter. I wanted you to have this."

"What about — my jewel fish?"

"Even your jewel fish," he confirms.

Plum looks down at the television, runs her fingers over its rounded crown. Its cost has reached into the clouds. She thinks of Cydar's quiet, watchful ways; and knows why he's done this sacrificial thing, and hates everything about the reason. "I'm sorry," she says.

From the security of the wall he considers her flushed face, her downcast eyes, her limp but stolid limbs. "It's all right. It'll be good. Life is change, Plum."

"I know," she says. "I'm glad. I'm glad I'm not a shovel-nosed catfish who ate the dinosaurs."

He smiles, and almost laughs, which is the greatest of the rare honors he bestows. He doesn't kiss her cheek, or ask if she likes the television, or give her instructions on its use or describe how he plans to fill his fishless days — but as he leaves the room on soundless feet, Plum hears the things he *could* say. And she feels the wrongness of loving Justin too much, and of never loving Cydar enough. She swallows hard, cradles the television to her, squeezes her face to the set's own. The world is such a sad kind place that she is forced to groan.

David is fractious. Maureen has bathed him and dressed him in fresh pajamas, and put him into bed surrounded by a frieze of trapeze artists and dancing poodles and pixies driving snub-nosed cars, but he will not close his eyes. His bedroom is lit by a nightlight, a teddy bear crowds his pillow, his truck is parked in its corner where he can see it, and yet he will not sleep. His eyes fly open the instant they close, his fingers twist the hem of the sheet. A frown has cut into the pale skin between his brows. His gaze leaps around like a frantic bird, touching the toys he didn't choose for himself, the clothes he is told to wear. The rain hits the window in rhythmless gusts, stony against the pane. Maureen puts a hand to her child's forehead. "Go to sleep," she urges. He turns his head: "Daddy, Daddy," he sighs. All afternoon he has whimpered for his father, until the sound has become like the rub of a shoe against a stripped heel. Maureen knows she should leave him — close the door, play a record, put distance between herself and the boy — yet she makes no move to rise from the mattress. It's not that she doesn't want to be alone: aloneness presents itself like a rocking raft, something on which she can lie down in the knowledge that he is safe, and she is safe, and they will both sleep untroubled through the night. Maureen often thinks about this raft, which is sometimes a cradle, sometimes a desert, sometimes the moon or the sea, not in order to escape herself, but so she might be escaped from. There is something in Maureen that's too worrying to put into words, something formless like the unseen presence that brushes past in the ocean. Something unsettling, but also pleasant. It is this that's keeping her here in the room, this underlying wrath. It does not want quenching, peace is its enemy. It wants to rake and rake over the hot coals of the day, growing larger and angrier and more uncontainable. Maureen strokes her son's forehead and tries to catch his hand, saying, "Shush, shush, David," while, inside, the furious thing gnaws on the events of this day, on recollections of that atrocious girl.

There's no truth in what the girl had said; but there is.

It seems to Maureen that she'd only looked away for a minute, but when she looked back it was to find that her life had congealed. She had not realized it happened this way—that one only gets to make a handful of decisions before everything is decided, that every choice fuses a different choice into impossibility. Routes close, options shrivel, and it all happens without fanfare, simply day following day—until, suddenly, life is no longer pliable, and becomes like a frieze on a nursery wall, the same thing over and over. Maureen had not realized, and now she's paying for her ignorance. Her fault is that she'd thought life was fairer, more generous, less rigid, that's all.

"Where's Daddy?" asks the boy; "Shush," says Maureen. She's made of glass tonight—a very thin glass forced to contain a substance as repugnant as tar. "Shush," she murmurs, drawing her mouth into a smile, but his eyes are on her untrustingly. He is old enough to recognize the fury in her, but not old enough to stifle in himself the fear that fury feeds on. Usually he can hide under a table, in the garden, behind a door. Tonight he is trapped on the bed, which is barren despite the puffy pillows and the carnival-patterned sheets. "Daddy!" he pleads, and the word infuses his mother's face with a blackness that is terrifying, yet must also be a good thing: for although she hates him for his fretfulness, she loves him for it too, because she loves how angry his distress makes her feel. "Daddy," he says, and can't stop saying. "I want Daddy," pawing helplessly at the linen.

"I know. But Daddy isn't here. Only me."

The rain hits the window harder, making the boy catch his breath. Despite the bulk of his bedding, he is shivering with cold. Tears have dampened his eyes, and his gaze shines around the room, over books and shoes and building-blocks, past superheroes and their plastic cars. His breathing jerks and flutters, his toes wrestle beneath the sheets. "I want someone," he says, and Maureen has to smile. *I want someone.* The wretched cry of the species, born into it like a faulty gene.

She closes her eyes and lets her head sink until her chin touches her chest. She boards the raft and glides through a place that is uncluttered and plain as sand. She recalls Justin in glimpses, as if he's bound up in web. She doesn't doubt that the words sneered by the girl were exactly what Justin had said. *I don't love her, no. Why would I?* It's likely he'd been trying to protect Maureen, choosing words that would convince through their sheer brutality. He knows, after all, that she loves him with a deathless love, a love that *has not the option to die.* He knows how rare such love is, he wouldn't vandalize such a thing without cause. Nevertheless, there's truth in what he'd told the girl. There are *circumstances.* There are all her wrong decisions. If life were changeable, she would change these calcified choices into ones that make her not only desirable, but claimable. Pitiable, too. If Justin pitied her more, he would be here. If he could see that he, too, might make decisions he one day regrets, then he would have sympathy. If he could see past his confusion to realize that, without him, she has nothing, that he's abandoning her to *nothing* . . . then he would have compassion. That's all he needs to feel for her: a greater amount of pity.

"Daddy . . ."

"Daddy's not here, David."

"But I want Daddy! I want Daddy!"

She rocks on his bed, fingers pressing in her thighs. She is nursing an injury like the bloody-edged gouge torn from flesh by a bullet. She understands Justin's reasoning: he was trying to protect her. But in doing so he's injured her profoundly.

"I want Daddy," says David; "I know," sighs Maureen. One elegant hand reaches out to him, slides smoothly down his cheek. "I know what you want," she comforts him; but doesn't say that life rarely grants more than a taste of what's wanted, and never deigns to give everything needed. "Poor boy," she mutters, because it is impossible not to feel sorry for a child who has so much to learn about the niggardly nature of life. If she had the means to make things different for him, for herself, for her husband, for Justin, and even for that girl, then nothing would remain as it is. It strikes Maureen as a noble thing to wish for, the power to make everything endurable.

Her hand is weighing like a white sea-creature across the boy's face. "Shh," she says, needing to quiet him because in this moment she craves silence: a light which is almost celestial has begun to burn in her mind. Inside it she sees how few things are truly worth wanting. A bird asks for nothing but wings. Deafened by light, she hardly notices that her son is still; in this cold room of dancing dogs and cartwheeling clowns it's as if nothing has ever happened, and the rain has brought the unheard-of opportunity of beginning again.